Fire and Water

Hayley Long was born in Ipswich in 1971 – one year after *Fire and Water* was released. This is her second novel. Her first was *The World of Elli Jones* (Bastard Books, 2001). She now lives in Cardiff and sometimes plays records in cafés.

Fire and Water

Hayley Long

PARTHIAN

Parthian
The Old Surgery
Napier Street
Cardigan
SA43 1ED

www.parthianbooks.co.uk

First published in 2004
© Hayley Long 2004
All Rights Reserved

ISBN 1-902638-52-2

Editor: Gwen Davies

Quotations from 'Oh I Wept' on Fire and Water by Free
(Island Records), and from T Rex's 'Metal Guru' on The
Slider (EMI Records). Both with kind permission.

Cover design by Lucy Llewellyn
Printed and bound by Dinefwr Press, Llandybïe, Wales
Typeset in Matt Antique by type@lloydrobson.com

Parthian is an independent publisher which works with
the support of the Arts Council of Wales and the Welsh
Books Council

British Library Cataloguing in Publication Data – A
cataloguing record for this book is available from the
British Library

In memory of Paul Kossoff, 1950-1976,
and
the Wheatley family of Aberystwyth,
whose shop Music Warehouse intrigued me
for over a decade (sadly it is now boarded up).

Thank you to Graham, Kirsty, Beca, Gwen and Marc Bolan.

I take my seat on the train
And let the sun cover my pain
From tomorrow I'll be far away
Let the sun shine on another day.

Rodgers/Kossoff

Contents

I. Fire and Water

Total playing time: 33' 59"

F&W: 3'51" – the track that kicked it all off! Oh and did I ever tell you that you've got what it takes to make a poor man's heart break?

Doors pull together with a warning hiss and a moment later the tell-tale tremor breaks out from underneath my feet. In no time at all, it has worked its way up my shins, rolled across the ever-expanding terrain of my thighs and flooded over my chest. I hold especially still as the tickle trickles down my left arm and into the hand which is awkwardly trying to stop the contents of a polystyrene cup from spilling over into my lap. At some point, probably around Newtown, the tremor will have engulfed my whole head

1

and I will need to take a couple of strong painkillers. At some other point, later still, it will strike me that I have become oblivious to it even though the tilt of other people's coffee in other people's cups will tell me that it is still very much present. But by then, I won't care. It will be as if the vibration has always been there and I will be unable to remember what my life was like without it. That doesn't usually happen until I've gone at least as far as Wellington or Telford. Over two hours away. But for now, three sharp signals cut through the air and the train lunges forward, pulling me slowly away from Aberystwyth.

It is raining. It often is. I've been making this journey for almost thirteen years and rarely have I pulled in or out of Aberystwyth without the rain pissing down on me. I prefer it that way. It means I know where I am. Some things never change.

I've always collected things. When I was eight, it was rubbers. All sorts of rubbers in all different colours. I catalogued them carefully and wrote a description of each one in my notebook along with the date and place it was purchased and the price I paid. I had a whole book filled with information like:

- _Item number 70_ – Mini hamburger rubber (smells of sick). 22p. Grange Road Post Office. 2nd May 1980.
- _Item number 71_ – Lime green Bugs Bunny rubber (smells like a sleeping bag). 36p. Shop in Cornwall. 12th June 1980 – my birthday!

● *Item number 72 – Shakin' Stevens rubber*
  – square block showing a picture of Shaky in
  a bright pink jacket (no smell). Swapped with
  Samantha Ruddock on the 21st June 1980 for
  the Union Jack flag rubber (smells of chicken)
  – see Item number 41.

At the height of my rubber fetish, I owned no less than 126 different rubbers but only four of them were actually capable of rubbing anything out. My mum took the collection away from me when I choked on *Item number 14,* my ice-cream-cone rubber which smelt like juicy-fruit chewing gum. This happened on October 8th 1980. I know because I recorded it in my book.

After that, I must have sensed a danger in actual *things* and I began to collect facts. For years and years I collected them and nobody even seemed to notice what I was up to. I knew everything. I knew that Ali Parvin was a great Egyptian footballer in the Seventies. I knew that rats were incapable of throwing up. I knew that a *fugleman* was a soldier placed at the front of a regiment and I knew that William Shakespeare and Manuel de Cervantes shared the same birthday. I also knew that I had no idea at all who Manuel de Cervantes was. But that didn't put me off. I read dictionaries and encyclopaedias and then I read Trivial Pursuit game cards and memorised the questions and when I had finished doing that I'd play for hours in my bedroom taking on the roles of all six opponents at once and I'd win hands down every time. On the rare occasions when my family switched off the television set and joined me in a game, I would tremble with excitement and race through the carefully stored answers in my head so I could show them what I had learned.

'OK then, Miss Clever-clogs, for your sixth piece of pie and for the title of Trivial Pursuit Champion Extraordinaire, here is your final question.' My father would dramatically pull a question card out of the box and hold it aloft in front of him for a second before pulling a sympathetic face, 'You'll never know this one.'

'I might,' responded the eleven year old version of me, indignantly. 'Just read me the question.'

'Who wrote *The Illustrated Man*?'

I'd huff and puff for a bit and mutter, 'Illustrated man? Illustrated man?' under my breath over and over again, my eyes screwed shut with feigned concentration, before tentatively asking, 'Ray Bradbury?'

Dad, amazed and trusting, began to look upon me as a child prodigy. My mum only shook her head in disapproval and said I should try to get out more.

By the time I got around to my O' Levels I was bored of collecting facts and wanted to get out more. The only trouble was I'd spent the past eight years reading encyclopaedias and dictionaries and Trivial Pursuit question cards so I didn't really have anyone that I could go out with. So I did the next best thing. I stayed in my room and listened to the radio and let the world come to me. And every Sunday evening, just after the chart countdown had finished, came the most exciting visitation of them all. *The Annie Nightingale Request Show*. I sat and listened and listened and then I began to make some lists in a notebook. The Undertones. The Doors. Lloyd Cole. The Damned. Anything I enjoyed got written down into the notebook. I soon had a whole book filled with information like:

- *'Stories of Johnny', Marc Almond* – released 1985 – played by Annie at 8:17 on 8th March 1987.
- *'She's not there', The Zombies* – released 1964 – first track played by Annie on 26th April 1987 (Annie said 'Hi' about four seconds into the intro).
- *'Fire and Water' by Free* (a very very good record! – taken from the 1970 album of the same name) – never released as a single (tragically) – played by Annie at 8:42, 3rd May 1987.

And that was how I got started on my greatest and most dearly loved collection of all. Vinyl. When CDs came along, everybody said that vinyl was dead. They were so wrong.

At Borth, somebody is waiting on the platform. I wipe the window and study this Borth-dweller with interest. In nearly thirteen years, I have never known anyone to get on or get off at Borth. I had come to assume that the place was empty. It occurred to me once that even the name of this place is indicative of desolation and inactivity. Whereas Aberystwyth is the sound of a vibrant and varied carnival across the eardrums, Borth is the sound of a slow puncture. Or flatulence. This Borth-dweller is a woman. She is dressed quite bizarrely in walking-boots and a long tasselly-skirt which has little mirrors sewn into the fabric. Up above, she is wearing a military coat that has a German-army flag sewn on to the sleeves. Perhaps she is a hiking hippy from Hamburg? My guess, however, is that she bought this coat in Aberystwyth. Aber's a great place for shopping if you want to buy coats like this. Even though her hair blazes red with henna, the lines around her eyes show she is some years older than me. She turns her head and I look down at my feet but it is too late. She has seen me looking. She pushes the button to release the doors and steps into my carriage. I am a little annoyed by this because I was enjoying having the entire carriage to myself but I knew that the odds were even as soon as I saw her there. After all, she only had one other carriage to choose from. This is hardly the Orient Express. Borth Woman shakes droplets of water from her hair like a dog and sits down on the seat just opposite mine. I breathe out slowly and shift my legs.

'Is this the train for Shrewsbury?'

I nod politely and quickly turn back to the window. The question might seem harmless but it is not. It tells me that Borth Woman is a nutter. Only one road exists in Borth and the solitary train track runs parallel to it and past a double-headed arrow which indicates, very clearly, the answer to her question.

Shrewsbury ←————→ *Aberystwyth*

And besides, anyone living in Borth must surely be aware of all the escape routes. Avoiding any more eye contact, I rummage in my bag and pull out my walkman so that I won't have to speak to her. She is quite obviously mad and it's anyone's guess what she is doing on a train at twenty past five on a Saturday morning.

On the other side of the glass, Borth's solitary street has been left behind and the Dyfi Estuary floats by. I can see miles and miles of water with no hint of a train track anywhere. For a second I fear that I might be feeling sea-sick but I sternly remind myself of how many more hours of this I have left to endure and forbid myself from entertaining such thoughts. I tell myself that I am not floating or drifting but that I am swimming very very fast and that I can put down my foot and touch the earth anytime I want to. I sneak a look at Borth Woman. She has taken a book out of her bag and is already reading it. *A Complete Guide to Middle Earth*. I turn back to the view and snort against the glass in disgust. She is evidently one of those people who sits and reads about imaginary lands filled with inhospitable landscapes and strangely-named people when the duplicated reality is scrolling past her unnoticed. If I lived in Borth I'd probably want to escape into fantasy as well but my fantasy would be distinctly urban. Gotham City or Metropolis, perhaps.

Not that I don't love this place. Growing up where I did, I appreciate the harsh lines and edges more than anyone. I could never sit and read a book whilst all this is going past me. It would be a waste. I have a book in my bag, of course, but I will wait until I'm in England before I actually attempt to read any of it. I also have a walkman, several tapes and a Gameboy and I refuse to use any of them just yet either.

The pattern in the tremor changes and I notice that we

are slowing down ready to make our stop at Dyfi Junction. I sneak another glance at Borth Woman to check that she is not watching me and then I very slowly inhale a long deep breath of air. Brakes squeal and the train grinds to a halt. I sit perfectly still, my chest raised, my lungs expanded. On the other side of the window, the empty shelter throws out its menacing challenge. I run my eye over the bust-up seats inside and hold myself absolutely immobile. Borth Woman turns a page of her book. A seagull lands and perches on top of the shelter. In my head I am counting elephants. *Seven elephants, eight elephants, nine elephants.* Waves ripple across the surface of the estuary. *Nineteen elephants, twenty elephants, twenty-one elephants.* The sorry shell of a fishing boat rises out of the mud and long grass at an uncomfortable angle. *Twenty-eight elephants, twenty-nine elephants, thirty elephants.* I wonder why the fisherman never came back to rescue his boat. *Forty-two elephants, forty-three elephants, forty-four elephants.* My chest is beginning to hurt me now. Far off in the distance, a vehicle is making its way along a hillside road. *Fifty-six elephants, fifty-seven elephants, fifty-eight elephants.* I wish the train would hurry up and move on because I can't hang on for much longer. Borth Woman turns another page. I can feel my head begin to spin. I blow a little air out through my mouth and stare at my feet. The engine rumbles back into life. *Thank God.* I make another measured expulsion of air. Finally, sparking within me a moment of intense joy, the signals sound and we pull slowly off again. With a rush of relief, I let go of the remainder of air and breathe in and out quickly a few times to dispel the dizziness. Tiny lights are dancing around in front of my eyes. Out of the corner of my eye, I think I see Borth Woman giving me a funny look so I make a little show of coughing as if I have a cold and then turn back to the scenery and watch Dyfi Junction disappear behind me.

I have never breathed at Dyfi Junction. Not once. In nearly thirteen years. As soon as I saw the place I had serious doubts about it. I was eighteen at the time; a new student at the university. I sat on the train that was taking me home for Christmas and I took one look at that lonely Portacabin in the middle of Middle Earth and I held my breath. Maybe it was the smashed-up seats inside the shelter or maybe it was just the fact that there was no other sign of human life in any direction for miles. Either way, I was so aghast at the idea that anyone could be expected to sit in this vulnerable little bubble waiting for their connecting train to take them to Aberdyfi or Barmouth or Harlech or wherever – whilst all of the time praying that the train would arrive before the mad axe-man who surely roamed these wilds did – that my breath was taken quite away. And since that first time, I've always felt that it would be unlucky to breathe in that place. So I haven't. It goes without saying that I've never experienced the delights of alighting at Dyfi Junction. Not even I, with all the practice I've had, could hold my breath for that long. Which is a shame, I suppose, because I've always quite fancied seeing the castle at Harlech. I'm still waiting for the day when I meet someone who can take me up in a car. But unless he's willing to drive a very long distance, I don't suppose that's likely to happen now.

The first time that I saw Jonny, he was sat behind the wheel of an enormous and ancient Mercedes Benz that had been festooned all over with crudely fashioned triangles sprayed in varying shades of metallic paint. It looked as if he'd accidentally driven into a pre-school picnic trip and been ambushed by three year olds wielding triangular-shaped potato printers. No doubt the purpose behind this enterprise had been to turn the heads of passing pedestrians and to this end, the operation had been successful. It caused my head to turn, if only to stand amazed at the unrivalled vulgarity of the owner's taste in cars. The man himself was stuck in traffic at the bottom of Penglais Hill and seemed oblivious to the look of horror he was receiving from the near-side pavement. It was a hot day and he had his window wound right down so that he could slap out on the side of the car door the bassline of something that was playing on his stereo. His blond hair was tied back in a messy pony-tail and he possessed the kind of cheek-bones which are almost always accompanied by a cocky personality. On first impressions, he didn't impress me. I liked my men dark and I liked my cheekbones hairy. Even with his long hair, this man in the terrible car was more Jason Donovan than Jim Morrison. I waited patiently, wanting to cross the road when it happened. Fate intervened. If the tape in my walkman had not expired at just that moment, I would never have bothered to give him a proper look. One second I was listening to the closing chords of *Sally Cinnamon* and the next, my play button had snapped upwards and I was sharing the sounds that were coming out of the triangle-infested Mercedes. *Fire and*

Water by Free. An Annie Nightingale favourite. Title track from the album of the same name. A very *very* good record! Never an obvious choice in 1989 – at the tale end of the *so-called* Second Summer of Love – but most definitely one for the connoisseur. My walkman forgotten, I stared at the profile of the driver of the most horrible car in Aberystwyth and decided that I wanted him.

It was the car that helped me get him. Despite my initial contempt for its triangles and colour schemes, I soon grew to be as fixated with the car as I was with its owner. Throughout the whole of my first year, I followed the car all over Aberystwyth in the hope that it would reveal more of the secrets of its Free-loving, floppy-haired, smooth-cheekboned driver. And it had done. Via the car, I had been able to learn that its owner was also a student at the university (no surprises there, admittedly) probably studying International Politics (the car was frequently parked close to the Interpol building) and most definitely living in a large ugly house at the end of Llanbadarn Road. Through my own further investigations – which usually opened with the line, 'You know that bloke who drives the weird Mercedes...?' I also discovered that his name was Jonny, that he was in his second year and that he enjoyed a certain amount of celebrity as the lead guitarist and singer of the student band, Mr Big. But only in Aberystwyth.

So when, at the end of my first year, I finally got the chance to talk to him, I felt like I had won two prizes. Jonny *and* the car. And in a town where the nearest big neighbour is a two-hour train ride away, that additional bonus was no small thing. As soon as that front passenger seat became mine, I stopped caring about the triangles outside. In fact, I even added a few more of my own.

I first met Jonny the evening after an Aber Beer Festival. As far as alcohol consumption was concerned, the beer festival had been a fairly moderate affair. Most of the alcohol in the Student Union had been spat into the faces of friends rather than actually swallowed. Too drunk to realise that I needed to change my beer-sodden clothes but too sober to go home to bed, I walked down the hill with my friends in search of some more entertainment. Our walk took us into The Central, then The Crystal Palace, then The White Horse and then along the seafront where I caused my whole company to come to a crashing halt behind me. Pinned up inside the window of The Bay was a fly poster:

Bands in the Bay

Tonite

The

Thora

Hurd

Experience

MR BIG

Not The Comfy Chair!

Tristan and the Killer Toasters

I tapped the poster with my finger. 'I want to go in.'

My friends stood around me in a group with uncertain faces. Kate, a nice girl from my course who – despite being wealthier than the rest of us put together – was so careful with her money that she had the reputation of being tighter than two coats of paint, looked at the poster doubtfully. 'It's three pounds just to get in. I don't think I can afford that. Can you afford that, Suzie?'

Suzie, a drama student with a taste for outdoor sex – apparently – and a more obvious tendency towards throwing tantrums, shrugged her shoulders elaborately and shook her head with painful regret. 'Not really. I'm trying to cut down on my spending. The Bank Manager made me cry last week. He was awful. He wanted to know what kind of books it is that I buy from Dorothy Perkins.'

I looked back at my so-called friends and stamped a Doctor Marten irritably on the pavement. 'You're trying to save? Oh, *now* you tell us! You've just spent at least fifteen pounds up in the beer festival and you had a bottle of Diamond White in The Central and another two in The White Horse *and* you fed loads of fifty pees into the juke box. What harm is another three quid going to do you?'

My friends pulled sulky faces and looked at each other for support. Suzie nominated herself as their spokesperson. 'I'm not being funny but who the hell are The Thora Hurd Experience, anyway? They sound like a bunch of old ladies. I don't want to see a bunch of old ladies playing guitars for three pounds, thank you very much.' Suzie glared back at me defiantly and my other so-called friends nodded their heads.

'Oh my God!' I screeched. 'I couldn't care less about the Dora Turd Experience or whatever the hell they're called. It's *him* I want to see. Mr Big. You know? The guy with the car?'

'Oh, *him*!' The words shot like wounding bullets. Suzie looked around at the others who, taking their lead from her, began to roll their eyes in exaggerated expressions of boredom. There was a definite sense of unified dissent amongst the ranks now. I could feel that I was losing the fight.

'To be honest, I think we're all quite bored of having our social lives fitted in around possible sightings of this Jonny-man. I can't speak for the others,' – well that was a lie for a start – 'but I think I've seen all the rubbish rock bands that I ever want to see. So, I don't mind what the rest of you do but I'm going on for a quiet pint in The Seabank.'

That was another lie. There was no such thing as a quiet pint in The Seabank. There was always, at the very least, blisteringly loud music or a fight going on in there. Or both, on a good night. Suzie made off down the sea front. Our friendship stormed off in the direction of the sea where it promptly drowned itself. I didn't really care. She had always been a bit too overly-dramatic for my liking. Another friend followed her, leaving the remainder of our little crowd still hovering uncertainly around the poster.

'It's only three quid,' I said, looking at Kate as my final hope, 'I'll pay.'

'Don't be silly. You can't afford to pay for all of us. And anyway, three quid is three pints if The Seabank still

15

has its offer on.'

My frustration burst its banks again. 'Oh, if if if. If your aunt was a man she'd be your uncle. And anyway, you don't need cheap alcohol to have a good time, you know.'

I could tell that I had really lost the argument now.

Kate smiled apologetically. 'We're going to The Seabank. Are you coming with us?'

'No.'

'See you then.'

'See you.'

An awkward silence descended as Kate and her companions turned to leave.

'Kate?'

'What?'

'Thanks for not being horrible to me.'

'Hey, no problem.'

'See you, then.'

'Bye.'

Feeling something that may have been a pang of regret, I watched the last of my friends abandon me and then pushed open the door of The Bay with renewed vigour. By refusing to go to The Seabank, I had unintentionally placed all my eggs in one basket. I needed to make this night count.

Downstairs in the Band Basement, I discovered that The Thora Hurd Experience were already on the stage and that the time was much later than I'd thought. It cheered me up a little to think that Suzie, Kate and the others had probably missed out on the 'pound a pint before ten at night' offer after all. Ignoring Thora and his chums who were dressed in orange caftans and doing their thing on a make-shift stage in the corner, I quickly surveyed the room and saw Jonny's blond head lying on one side on the bar. I walked over and sat on the stool next to him. Jonny's eyes were shut and there was a pint glass of snakebite and black positioned just in front of his nose. I pulled the sleeve of a young man with a shaved head who was standing just next to Jonny and who I recognised as a guitarist in Mr Big.

'Is he all right?' I said, indicating Jonny.

The man with the shaved head turned and looked at me with surprise and then looked at Jonny and said, 'Him? He's fine. Just a bit pissed off.'

He had a South Walian accent and was wearing a T-shirt with a picture of Fireman Sam on the front. For some reason, this appealed to me. If I had been a woman of lesser focus I may, perhaps, have gone for him. Instead, I looked back at Jonny.

'Pissed off? He looks pissed to me.'

'No, he's not pissed. He's just a moody git, that's all. I'm Rhys, by the way, can I get you a drink?'

Before I could answer, Jonny – my Jonny – suddenly raised his head from the bar and rounded on Rhys.

'Oy, who are you calling a moody git, you crusty old bastard?'

'You!' Rhys's attention was fully on Jonny now and he seemed to have forgotten his offer to buy me a drink.

'Me?'

'Well you are. You were in a strop all the way through our set. You didn't even put any energy into *Latvian Lovers* and that's supposed to be our show-stopper. We'll never get

17

to headline if you sing like that. You were shite. And all because you chucked your teddy out of your pram when Thora got the top billing. Poor little Jonny-diddums.'

Jonny scowled. It was a beautiful high cheek-boned, blond-haired kind of a scowl. 'Fuck Head.'

Rhys laughed delightedly and then grabbing Jonny's head between his hands, planted a big smacking kiss on the centre of his forehead. 'We love each other really,' he said to me with a wink and then turned back to his other friends, the offer of a drink still forgotten. Jonny pouted and reached for his pint of snakebite. He downed half in one and then paused as if a sixth sense had warned him that somebody was staring at him very closely.

Somebody was. Me.

'Hello,' he said eventually after staring back at me uncertainly for a few seconds.

'Hi.'

'Did you like the gig?'

'Oh yeah. Actually I only came to see your band. That's why I'm not watching this lot now. I don't really rate them.'

'Oh.' Jonny sucked in his cheekbones and appeared to think deeply about this for a moment. Whatever conclusion he came to was obviously a favourable one because eventually, he added, 'I'm Jonny. Do you want a drink?'

This was one offer of a drink that I was determined would not get forgotten.

'Thanks, yeah. Bottle of DW, please.' I frowned and raising a hand to my ear, said a little louder, 'Sorry, what did you say your name was?'

'Jonny.'

'Ronny?' This was fun.

'No. *Jonny*.' He passed me an opened bottle of Diamond White. I smiled, took a long swig and prepared to hit him with my secret weapon.

'I was wondering, *Jonny*, did you name your band after track five on Free's 1970 album, *Fire and Water*?'

Jonny looked at me blankly for a split-second as if his brain needed a moment to digest the question and then his face broke out into an amazed smile and he leant forward so that he could deliver the answer personally to my ear.

I don't know how long we talked about Free and I don't remember how many more bottles of Diamond White I drank that night. But I do know that pretty soon Jonny's mouth moved around from my ear to my lips and I do know that his kiss was worth every second of the eight months I had waited for it. He may have been second billing at The Bay Hotel but he snogged like a stadium rock star. I also know that the three quid I had paid on the door was the best three quid I had ever spent.

2. Oh I Wept

4' 25" Beautiful lyrics, beautiful axe work!

For all my good intentions of enjoying the scenery one last time, I must have fallen asleep. I have snoozed through the opportunity to say a final farewell to Machynlleth and Caersws. Troubled by this, I bite my lip. The train is now stationary by the platform in Newtown and a young man still in his teens and wearing a cheap suit has joined us. He pulls a copy of *Kerrang!* magazine from a pocket and sits down to read it. I sneak a look at the front cover with interest but I'm disappointed to see that I do not recognise the scowling cover stars. This doesn't really surprise me. I have let my music knowledge slip in recent years. I've had no choice but to let it slip, really. It's all a matter of quality control and these modern 'skate-rock' outfits simply do not reach the exacting standards of my listening specifications. In a word, they are shit. Every day when I was at work, I used to watch all the students wandering about looking younger every year and marvelled at how completely crap the names on their T-shirts were. Limp Bizkit. Blink 181. Alien Ant Farm. System of a Down. *System of a Down?* Every day, I sat on my stool behind the high desk, stamping books which I had borrowed myself years before and I had pitied them in their stupid T-shirts. I'm glad I won't be doing that anymore.

Opposite, I see that Borth Woman is still with me. Her nose is still buried deep up Gandalf's backside and she has a little notepad balanced on her knee into which she is scribbling notes. I raise my eyebrows a little cynically. Obviously Borth Woman has taken this whole Tolkien thing a little too far.

The train rumbles back to life and we pull away from Newtown. Despite its name, I know for a fact that Newtown is actually quite an old town. I know that it is the home of the first WH Smiths. I know that there is a small art gallery and a nice pub called The Lion Inn where Jonny and I once sat and I had drunk whisky and cokes for an entire afternoon and Jonny had only pretended to because he was driving. I know probably all there is to know about Newtown. Not many people would bother to make it the destination for a day-trip but Jonny and I did. Although that was only because he didn't have enough petrol or enough money to get us as far as Shrewsbury and back. When we had got back to the car someone had left a post-it note stuck to the windscreen with the words *I'll buy this car off you for 50p* written on it. Jonny said that whoever wrote that had a cheek because it was worth at least seventy-five.

In spite of myself, I feel my eyes moisten. I knew this journey would not be easy and thinking about Jonny is not helping to make it any easier. I look at my watch. It is a quarter past six. Studying my time-table, I see that in an hour's time, I will be somewhere between Shrewsbury and Wellington. This thought cheers me up. I really will be on my way then. And if I'm still feeling morose, at least I'll be in the heart of the Black Country and will have a reason to feel bad.

I pull my Gameboy out of my bag and switch it on. I need something to occupy my mind. Out of the corner of my eye, I spot the head of the *Kerrang!* reader stiffen and look over towards me with interest. I press the buttons of my Gameboy and pretend that I am playing *Lamborghini American Challenge* but really, I am not. I have already found a much more interesting game to play. I am creating a whole new life for the *Kerrang!* boy. I have decided to call him Newton, after the town he lives in. Newton Spots – he has quite a few of these on his face. Newton is young, eighteen at the most and he works for a cowboy insurance company in Shrewsbury. They make him do all the shitty jobs like getting the tea and filing and shredding the evidence and they pay him hardly anything. Not even the minimum wage because Newton isn't officially on the company books. But he doesn't care because there's nothing much to do every day in Newtown and this way he gets to wear a suit and be a commuter and learn the ropes of selling dodgy insurance policies. And for the record, he doesn't care that his suit looks cheap. In fact, he isn't even aware of it.

In almost no time at all, the train is pulling in at Welshpool and I'm starting to feel really worried about young Newton Spots. He looks so innocent sat there with his head buried in his music magazine. He looks as if he's just playing the part of an adult but the role, like the suit, is a little bit too big for him. He is looking out of the window with an anxious expression and I am sure that he is, like me, worrying that the train is taking him closer to Shrewsbury and that office where he works and gets exploited on a daily basis. I stare hard into the screen of my Gameboy and think about leaning over to him and telling him to shove the job up his boss's arse and go home again. Jobs like that, where you spend most of your time sitting still and talking all day whilst actually having meaningful conversations with no one, wear you down after a while. And if anybody should know that, of course, I bloody should after the nine and a half years I spent stamping those damn books in the Hugh Owen Library. I'm right on the brink of telling Newton this when he does something that I am really not expecting. He stands up, stuffs his magazine into a pocket and gets off the train. Outside, another young man in an equally cheap suit and an older man with a bushy beard who can only be the former's dad, are standing on the platform waiting. As Newton joins them, the older man pats him affectionately on the shoulder and the younger man gives him a big excited grin. Before the doors slide shut, I hear a snatch of their conversation and catch just enough to be able to guess that the two young men are off to visit a university they both hope to attend next year. The older man is driving them. Newton Spots (although now I see that this is probably not his name) does not work for a company of cowboy insurance salesmen in Shrewsbury after all. He is a nice boy who wants to continue his education. I am relieved. I am even more relieved that I never talked to him about his job prospects.

Jonny *never* had a job. Not once during the whole time I knew him. Jonny reckoned that having a job was just another form of prostitution. 'Selling your body or selling hours of your young life?' he once asked me. 'Hours which you can never have back. Which is the bigger horror?' I had a Saturday job at the time, selling rucksacks and walking boots in Cheapy Charlie's in town and although I didn't enjoy it all that much, I was sure that it couldn't be as bad as giving a blow-job to a desperate saddo on the backseat of an Astra down some dark alleyway. I told Jonny this and he said that I had been sucked in by the fallacy that was capitalism and consumerism. I said that as long as capitalism and consumerism meant that all I had to do for my money was bring out the odd pair of size nines from the stock-cupboard, I didn't mind. But as soon as it meant giving the odd sixty-nine to someone willing to pay that bit extra then I was out of there. Jonny said that when I was old and wrinkly and on my death bed, I'd regret the time I'd wasted selling walking boots in Cheapy Charlie's and would be ready to give anything for the odd sixty-nine in the back of an Astra. I said, 'OK then. I'll ask Rhys and the other band members if any of them would be interested in paying me for a few special services. The money would come in handy.' Jonny said, 'You bloody well will not!' and then sulked for the rest of the day. In spite of his prettiness, Jonny could be a real prat sometimes.

But that didn't mean that I adored him any less. During the whole of my second and third year, Jonny and I were inseparable. My first year friendships had been terminally cooled by the incident outside the Bay Hotel so I had few qualms about moving out of the eight foot by six foot prison cell I had occupied in a hall of residence up on the campus. At least it meant that I'd never again have to listen to the audio effects of Suzie's increasingly adventurous sex experiments through my paper-thin walls. Armed with my collection of suede jackets and Doctor Martens, I moved into the big ugly house on the end of Llanbadarn Road and kept Jonny company while he wrote his songs and dreamed about the day when Mr Big would dominate the whole of the world's rock and pop scenes. During the week, I dragged myself out of bed and attended lectures on Middle English Romances and eighteenth century novels and on Saturdays, I stumbled, all hungover, to Cheapie Charlie's to sell rucksacks and walking boots. But apart from that, we were always together. And it seemed to me like that was just the way it was supposed to be.

I keep my eyes wide open and try to take in everything that is rushing by on the other side of the window. These will be my last glimpses of Wales. Possibly forever. I don't want to miss anything. I want to try and hold on to these final minutes of my life in Wales. The closing minutes of almost thirteen years. Back then, when I had arrived all fresh-faced and barely turned eighteen, I could never have guessed that the tiny town of Aberystwyth would suck me in for so long. It does that to some people. They arrive and they never leave. Or not without a struggle anyway. My life in Wales proved to be longer than the whole of the Beatles' recording career and it was a good match too for the Iron Lady's reign of terror. Not even the Stone Roses hung about in Wales for as long as I did. I could have made *The Second Coming* a second time in the years that I had. And a third and fourth coming.

Borth Woman is not looking out of the window. She is still reading her book and scribbling from time to time in the notepad. Obviously she doesn't care that at any moment now we are about to leave Wales and enter England. I look around the carriage at the other passengers. There aren't many of us. I suppose that most people are not up yet. I wouldn't be normally. On Saturdays, I tend to be more of a pm person. Across the aisle and sitting by the opposite window is a man of about my age. He is wearing combat trousers and a fleece top and when I look at him carefully, I see that he is actually quite ruggedly handsome. But even so, I could never fancy him. I am completely turned off by the way he is eating his apple. He is taking teeny-weeny bites at it like a hamster but still managing to make quite a noise, even above the rattle of the train. I cross my fingers down the side of the seat and hope that he's going to get off at Shrewsbury. His apple finished, he looks about for a bin and then, not seeing one, places the core on a paper tissue on the seat beside him so that we now have a browning apple core between us. Irritated, my eyes flicker about the carriage but again come to rest on the offending article on the seat just across the aisle.

In my collection, I had several Apple records. The Beatles of course, but also some John Lennon solo singles and a couple of albums by the Welsh rockers, Badfinger. As much as anything, I liked these records for their aesthetic quality. The big apple in the centre of the label – shiny and green on Side A but cut in half to reveal its core on Side B – was a distinctive trademark of quality and as far as I was concerned, no small print was needed. The apple told me all that I needed to know and my ears could work out the rest. My dad, who had been wholly uninterested in the collection of rubbers that I had amassed as an eight year old, was much more encouraging and appreciative of this new collection and often contributed items of rarity or other note on Christmases and birthdays. It was he who had given me all my Apple records, telling me that if I was going to clog up my bedroom with cumbersome LPs and 45s then I might as well have something worth listening to amongst it all. This remark had come soon after I had purchased my first Smiths record and treated my family to a non-stop airing of *Heaven Knows I'm Miserable Now* for the following fortnight. My father, despite his good taste in Apples, did not like The Smiths at all.

'Who is this?' he asked, only two hours into my

fourteen-day Smith-a-thon.

'The Smiths. Good, aren't they?'

'Good? It sounds like the singer is being disembowelled alive. I'd rather eat my own liver than listen to any more of this depressing dirge. Turn it off!'

I didn't turn it off but I did, grudgingly, turn it down a little.

When I left home, to go to university, I had to leave the records behind. I had tried to convince my mum that if I limited myself to no more than twenty LPs, we'd be able to fit them and a small turntable into the car but my mum said it was out of the question. When I'd cried and created a scene, she'd given way just enough to say that it was them or my Docs and suede jackets. Guessing that footwear and coats could well be essential items in the west of Wales, I'd finally relented and reluctantly agreed to leave the records behind.

It turned out that I had made the right choice. Jonny, who had driven himself in the Mercedes Benz with triangles, had brought his entire record collection with him. All three hundred and ten of them taking up ninety-three centimetres of shelf space. And from the moment of our first snog at the end of my first year, I had unlimited access to the whole lot. Mercifully, Jonny *did* like The Smiths. And Lloyd Cole and The Doors. And some new ones which he introduced me to – Elvis Costello and Television and PJ Harvey. But most of all, he liked Seventies rock – David Bowie, T Rex, Golden Earring, Free, Heart, Lynyrd Skynyrd... and everything was arranged alphabetically on his record shelves just like I would have wanted it to be.

It was through his record collection that I was really introduced to the other band members. It was one of those lovely rainy afternoons in the early days of our romance and Jonny and I were in his bedroom drinking sherry and pulling record after record from the shelf and playing each other snippets of our favourite tracks.

'Listen to this,' Jonny said, slipping a copy of *The Slider* out of its cover and placing it on the turntable. 'I love T Rex. There will never ever be another lyricist like Marc Bolan. Not even Rodgers and Kossoff matched him. He was the man. He was the Bolan Child. He was fantastic.' He turned the bass volume down to zero so that Marc Bolan's voice and incredible talent for writing song lyrics could best be appreciated. I sat and listened, sipping my sherry and nodding my head in time with the music.

> *Metal Guru*
> *Has it been*
> *Just like a silver-studded sabre-toothed dream.*
> *I'll be clean you know*
> *pollution machine, OH YEAH!*

'Fucking genius!' said Jonny, his eyes shut. 'Fifth of May, nineteen seventy-two, that was released. They don't write lyrics like that anymore.'

'*What's this!*' I said, putting down my glass of sherry and pulling records at random off the shelf. I knew very well what it was. It said so very clearly on the cover. But my exclamation was one of mischievous delight at finding something embarrassingly dreadful. In my hand I was holding a copy of *It's a Heartache* by Bonnie Tyler.

Jonny's face reddened rather a lot. 'It's quite good actually.'

'Bonnie Tyler? Are you serious?'

Jonny shrugged, then gave a little smile and then began to chuckle. 'Rhys gave it to me. We've got this thing going in the band where we share music so that we can understand where each other is coming from. Say for example that I get into something new, then I share it with the others. It keeps our listening experiences nice and wide and our tastes eclectic.'

I got the impression that he may have said these words before.

'Oh.' I nodded. 'Got any more Bonnie?'

'Yeah, I've got her whole back catalogue. Her recent stuff is really good.'

My eyebrows shot off the top of my head.

Jonny grinned. 'Only kidding, babe. Like I said, it's Rhys. He likes anything Welsh. I think he does it on principle. Some of the stuff he's given me is OK. There's this band from Cardiff called The Crumblowers who are quite good. They're like a Welsh Teenage Fanclub and the singer has got really mad hair which is always a good sign.'

'Except for Leo Sayer.'

'True.' Jonny drank some more sherry and looked again at the offending article in my hand. 'But then again, Rhys is also into The Alarm and they're shit. And then there's Bonnie Tyler and she's really shit.'

'You said she was quite good.'

31

'Yeah, well I lied.' Jonny leant forward and pulled another record from the shelf. *Jane Birkin and Serge Gainsbourg*. 'This,' he said, taking Marc Bolan off the turntable and replacing it with this new choice, 'is the choice of Waggy. Waggy is our bass player and he will only listen to stuff released between 1966 and 1974. He says everything before 1966 sounds primitive and everything after 1974 sounds pathetic. I don't quite agree with him because Blondie were brilliant for a start but I'm afraid he's not going to budge on this one.'

'Who did you say this was?' I asked, not recognising the sounds coming out of the speaker.

'Serge Gainsbourg. He's a French pervert. I'm not sure if he's still alive or not but I think his music is quite funky. Anyway, Waggy fancies himself as a bit of a Serge Gainsbourg character.'

'What? French and pervy?'

Jonny smiled. 'He tries. The perviness is not a problem but the French bit is harder. He comes from Swindon.'

'So what about your drummer?'

Jonny refilled our glasses with sherry and frowned. 'Now he's the one we really have to watch. Jeremy is a bit of a posh boy at heart and he's been brought up by trendy parents who fed him on a diet of contemporary jazz. So now, Jeremy has a taste for this jazz nonsense which is completely *not* rock and we have to watch him because sometimes he forgets that we're not called The Jeremy Evans Band and starts to do a bit of improvisation in the middle of one of our songs. He winds me up.'

I stood up and looked along the shelf for the Fs.

Finding our record exactly where it should be, I moved over to the turntable, brought the French Perv to a halt and listened to Paul Kossoff play his opening riff. I'd decided that I'd learned enough about the other band members and needed to know more about their lead singer. Placing my arms around Jonny's neck, I fluttered my eyelashes at him and turned on my best Dusty Springfield voice. 'If you're feeling all wound up, maybe I should help you wind down a little.'

From his response, I'd say that Jonny thought that was a good idea.

Three years later, watching Jonny pack those records into boxes was just as hard as watching the train that was taking him away from Aber and from me, disappear down the track forever. We were living in the flat in North Parade by then, just the two of us, and seeing him slowly, methodically empty our flat of all his things had been more than I could bear. In the end I had left him to it and walked around the town in the rain so that I wouldn't have to watch. My feet had carried me up towards Penglais Hill so that I could look in the window of Andy's Records and then I had walked on towards Aber's other, eternally closed, music shop where I had stared hopelessly at the window display and then burst publicly into tears before moving on again. I had cut back through town, down Pier Street and stood looking at the grey sea and sky, indistinguishable from one another and then walked back to find that all Jonny's stuff was in boxes waiting to be picked up by the delivery company. Jonny had left behind a note saying that he was staying with friends that night and that he would be leaving Aberystwyth on the first train out in the morning, if I wanted to come and say goodbye to him.

In spite of myself, I had gone. The next morning at five o'clock I had found him alone on the platform smoking a cigarette and looking sheepish. Whenever I have re-lived the moment in my head, I have made myself either aloof and uncaring or else blindingly furious but the reality was neither of those. I had walked across to him and smiled, a sad, resigned sort of a smile and he had put out his cigarette, enfolded me in his arms and given me a close lingering hug.

'Are you going to be OK?' he asked.

'I'll be fine.' The words sounded like they were coming from someone else.

'You're a really great girl. You'll soon forget about me.'

Stiffly, I pulled myself away from his embrace and looked him coldly in the eye. 'I already have.'

He blushed and kicked the butt of his cigarette with his boot. Then, giving me one last small smile, he picked up his bag and boarded the train. There were no tears or kisses from either of us, just a sense of time moving on. It wasn't until I was back, alone, in the flat that I allowed myself to cry and then I wept for days.

The houses are getting thicker and thicker and the hills have almost completely disappeared. The apple core is still on the seat across the aisle and the man who eats like a hamster is not making any attempt to collect his things together. With a sigh, I realise that our journeys are not yet ready to separate. Borth Woman also seems like she's staying put. I'm less bothered by this. In fact, we've come so far together now that I'm getting quite used to having her around. We are two little hobbits together venturing far, far away from Middle Earth. Outside, a platform emerges and races alongside the train until both it and the train stop altogether. I am in Shrewsbury or, for the benefit of those coming from the west, *Amwythig*. I am no longer in Wales and this is the last place I will pass through which can be expressed in the Welsh tongue. Finally, I have left Wales behind. My clothes are all bundled into the rucksack underneath my seat and now it is *my* books and other possessions which have been packed into boxes and will be delivered to my mum's address by a parcel company. My adult life in England begins right here, Shrewsbury station at – I check my watch – five minutes to seven on a Saturday morning. I am exactly thirty-one years old. I rummage in my bag and pull out a book. *No One Here Gets Out Alive – a biography of The Doors* – something I borrowed from the Hugh Owen Library and forgot to put back. I've read it at least once during the past decade but I saw it there on the shelf and fancied reading it again for some reason. I suppose I was just surprised that such a book existed in an academic library. Thanks to me, it doesn't anymore. I hold the book open in front of my eyes and stare blankly at the words on the page. To tell the truth, I don't really much like The Doors now – too much wailing and whining and not enough bass. But it doesn't matter anyway because I have no intention of reading this book.

I just need something to hide the fact that I am crying.

3. Remember

*4' 22" Has an air of Lennon and McCartney about it. A
great driving track – you, me, the Merc and the open road....*

The train has suddenly got much busier. Despite the fact
that it's still only seven in the morning, its two carriages
are now more than half full and the man who eats like a
hamster has moved his apple core on to the floor to create
an additional vacant seat. I am relieved about this because
I was worried that I might witness the entire process of
biological breakdown take place before my eyes and I'm
not sure if I could stand that level of excitement today.
Even though the apple core is no longer in my direct line of
vision, I can still smell its sweet and cidery presence. It
reminds me uncomfortably of all those mornings when I
have awoken ill with the sweat on my clothes generated by

too many bottles of Diamond White. Suddenly feeling claustrophobic and less than well, I delve once again into my bag in search of a couple of headache pills which I wash down with the cold remains of the cup of coffee that I bought almost two hours earlier from a vending machine on the platform at Aber.

I am not alarmed by my sudden illness; I was expecting it. It is always the same. At first, the novelty and excitement of the journey keeps my brain stimulated and the peace of my surroundings and the emptiness of the train as it winds its way from Cardigan Bay through central Wales brings me relaxation. But then we reach England and the geography changes and the people get more numerous and a headache sets in. I used to think that this was some kind of spiritual voice urging me to turn back and telling me that I belonged in Wales despite my background. Now I see that it is an essential pain barrier which I must pass through if ever I am to regain control of things and move on with my life. There is nothing much to look at anymore; all the panoramic scenery is well behind me. I will have to seek entertainment from another source. I put down the book I am holding but not reading and pull my walkman and a handful of tapes out of my bag. I only ever listen to my walkman when I feel the need to indulge myself. Usually, my whole head is a walkman. That is probably the reason why I only got a 2.2. When I sat in my final exam and searched for the reasons why William Shakespeare advocated a more orthodox morality than Christopher Marlowe, I found the words to *Maggie May* by Rod Stewart instead.

Right now, I need something relaxing to listen to which will not aggravate my head any further. I examine the tapes in my hand. *Jane's Addiction... The Very Best of The Cult... The Chemical Brothers.* Any of those would finish me off just at this moment. *Catatonia... Free.* I pull the inlay card out of *Free* and read the first line of a spidery and faded but all too familiar hand. *Fire and Water... the best rock album ever made and the album that brought you to me! Love forever, Jonny xxx.* I breathe out deeply, carefully replace the hand-made inlay and put this tape back into my bag. Despite its ever-present position amongst my tape cassettes, I have not listened to this one for years and I have no intention of listening to it now either. Which leaves me with only one option. I shove Catatonia into my walkman, press play and close my eyes as Cerys Matthews sings the opening lines of *You've Got a Lot to Answer For.*

At the foot of Penglais Hill, just a few doors up from Andy's Records, there is a shop which has acquired a mythical status. It is full of second-hand vinyl and songbooks and ancient yellowing posters and doubtless a million other things which I would like to own. During the whole of my thirteen years as an Aber resident, this shop was my own personal Pandora's Box. In it was everything I had ever wanted if only I knew how to open it. And that was just the problem: the shop was never open. This didn't mean that it had simply been abandoned and never cleared out, because clearly, somebody *did* oversee the shop. I knew this because the window display kept changing. Not obviously. An untrained eye could never have spotted it. As far as I

39

could tell, nothing ever got removed from the window but every so often, perhaps once every few months or so, something new would be added. A poster of Charlotte Church here. An album cover from Oasis there. To most people walking past, it probably seemed as if nothing in the window ever changed. But since I stopped and stared at least twice daily as I walked by, I knew better than this. It was clear that something was happening in the shop, it was just never at all clear when. Some of the things in the window looked as if they had been there from a time before I was born. A faded sticker on the glass advertised *National Record Tokens for Listening Pleasure* and a curling poster of Engelbert Humperdinck beamed smugly from the rear of the window display. When I cupped my hands together and peered through the glass and into the gloom, I could make out a cluttered and ancient shop counter adorned with boxes of Sixties music magazines and countless other bits of rock and pop junk. How I wanted to walk my fingers through those old magazines! But each time I tried the door, no matter what the time or day of the week, it was locked. Baffled, I read the many stickers and notices on the shop door to see if there was some clue as to when I could actually get in. There was no hint. Not a sign. The shop was always in darkness and I was perpetually disappointed.

Maybe, after my initial year of lingering longingly on the pavement outside the window, I might have got over it all and diverted my full attention to Andy's Records just a few doors down. But how could I? In pride of place, at the centre of the display and bleached almost to whiteness by years of exposure to the sunlight, was an original album cover of Free's *Fire and Water* signed by none other than the lead guitarist, Paul Kossoff. The signature, scrawled in the bottom right-hand corner in a spidery hand, was stubbornly refusing to fade at quite the same rate as the picture behind it. *Fire and Water* – a very very good record and the one which had brought me to Jonny. *And signed too.*

Wellington and Telford come and go with fewer than ten minutes between them. All the seats are full now and Borth Woman and I are sharing our seating area with two young women who got on at Telford. At a guess, I would put them in their early twenties because they look older and harder than any of the students I used to see wandering around the Hugh Owen Library but maybe they have just had tougher lives. They are both chewing gum and dripping gold. Both of them have their long hair scraped back from their foreheads so tightly that it looks painful. The one who is sitting next to Borth Woman has pink highlights in her blonde hair. She is the prettier of the two. The one sitting next to me looks like a bulldog. One which has had a spiral perm. I run my hand through my own hair. It's only about an inch long all over. I feel like a different species. The woman with the pink hair sees me looking and gives me a suspicious glare. She obviously feels the difference too. Quickly, I turn back to the window and try to decide the purpose of their journey. It is too early for them to be shopping and yet they are dressed too casually to be doing anything more important. Unable to help myself, I lean against the window, place my hand over my eyes as if I am dozing and study them through a narrow gap in my fingers.

For a reason that I do not understand, I am fascinated by them. The one with the pink hair stirs a cappuccino sulkily and flicks a contemptuous glance at Borth Woman's attire. Borth Woman is so deeply into her book that she is unaware of this and I am glad because she looks like the sensitive type. She probably had a tough time at school at the hands of girls just like these two.

The woman with the pink hair suddenly realises that I am watching her and gives me an unequivocal *what-you-staring-at?* type of glare. I give a slight jump in my seat, examine my hands very closely and then turn back to the safety of the window to try and spot the next iron horse galloping unconvincingly in 2D along the side of the train track. These horses are supposed to signify the industrial heritage of the Black Country. Iron cut-out Noddy Holders positioned every few miles or so along the track would have celebrated the area's true heritage. They would have given the passengers of these crappy trains something to smile about as well.

The two women from Telford are talking and I inconspicuously flick down the volume control button of my walkman so that I can listen to what they are saying. Their conversation is priceless. The one with the pink hair who hates me – I shall call her Donna Karan – is getting quite heated about some bloke called Terry and Bulldog is nodding her head vigorously and throwing in a fair few expletives in her support. Borth Woman is still reading about dragons and hobbits and scribbling in her note-book and seems unaware of the more earthy entertainment in front of her.

'So anyway, right, I said to Maxine that she was a silly tart to think that Terry would even look twice at her cos ee knows which side his bread is buttered and if ee can have a premier league bird like me, ee's hardly likely to go for an old Sunday League crow like her now, is he?'

'You're 'kin dead right there. Bang on. Did you say that to her? What did 'kin silly bitch say to that?'

'Hell knows? Just crawled off back to whatever cornflake packet it is that she lives in. And I shouted after her, I shouts "Stay away from my feller, you scrubber or I'll ave you," and I expected that to be an end to it.'

'Fuck, were it not?'

Bulldog leans in so that she can hear the rest of Donna Karan's story better and against my better judgement, so do I.

'Fuck were it! Guess who I sees propping up the bar in Cindy's Thursday night?'

'Terry!' I say inwardly.

'Terry!' says Bulldog outwardly.

'Yeah wi' that 'kin little slapper Maxine on his arm.'

'So what did you do?' I ask inwardly.

'Fuck! What d'you do?' asks Bulldog.

'Well, I goes marching over to the bar to have a go an' all and before I can even get a word in, Terry says... *my so-called Terry* says, "Well look if it int that two-timing easy little slag from Wolverhampton."'

'No!'

'Fuck!'

'So you know what I did?'

'What? What did you do?' I'm totally caught up in this

43

now, as is Bulldog who has her mouth open in a manner which is letting all her gorms escape.

'I take my pint – lager and a splash – and I tip it all over his soddin' head and then I says to im, "Do you mind? I'm not from fuckin' Wolverhampton, I'm from Telford, you twat." That fuckin' showed im.'

'FFNAAAAARRRGGHH!'

The conversation stops abruptly and Donna Karan, Bulldog and Borth Woman are all looking at me. Two of those faces look very cross. The third one is wearing an expression which is a perfect picture of both anxiety and amusement. With a terrible sickening sinking feeling of horror, it dawns upon me that the loud snort of laughter came from me. Sweating, I try to seek solace once again at the window but it is too late.

'Oy, what's your problem?'

Donna Karan is speaking to me. Horrified, I look up at her and give her a very scared smile.

'Was you laughing at us?'

I open my mouth to say something but as soon as my brain takes in the sight of her pursed lips and narrowed eyes, whatever it is that I wanted to say sails clean out of my mind. My jaw suddenly feels all slack and heavy so I mutely shake my head and desperately hope that this is not going to descend into violence. I know that I would not stand a hope in hell against either of these two.

In the seat next to me, Bulldog decides to have a turn. She clenches her fist on the table and says, 'Did you just call my mate a slag?'

Even more alarmed, I shake my head again. I've never

been in a physical fight in my entire life. I really don't want one now either. I thought that at thirty-one I was safely beyond all of this.

'Yeah well...' says Bulldog, jabbing her finger at me, 'you better not have done.'

Believing that she has put the fear of God into me – which to be perfectly honest, she has – Bulldog turns back to her mate and rolls her eyes in my direction.

Donna Karan mutters 'Lesbian!' just loud enough for me to hear and the two of them resume their conversation about Terry.

Shocked almost to a state of paralysis by my near-fight I sit and stare at the table and feel my cheeks burn through my bones. For once, it is Rhys that I miss and not Jonny. I'm sure that Rhys would know just what to do to stop myself from completely burning up. I wish I knew where he is now and what he is doing.

My thoughts are distracted by someone gently tapping my foot. I look up and stare right into the eyes of Borth Woman. Over the top of her book, she pulls a face in the direction of Donna Karan and Bulldog and gives me a secret grin. It takes a second or so for me to fully comprehend the bravery and selflessness of this kind act. When I do, I beam back at her and then, after checking that it is safe, pull a worse face in the direction of The Telford Two. Borth Woman bites her lip to stop herself from laughing. Much comforted and my confidence restored, I turn back to the window.

'Hey, guess what!'

I looked up from my essay and was greeted by the sight of Jonny, all out of breath and over-excited, leaning against the door-frame of the bedroom.

I put down my pen and sighed. It wasn't easy meeting the requirements of my course whilst living with a future rock mega-star who had already decided that he'd be perfectly happy with a 'Thora Hurd' degree and couldn't understand why I didn't feel quite the same way myself. Jonny always reckoned that our degrees would count for nothing when he had more money than Michael Jackson.

'This better be good, Jon. You know I've got to hand this essay in tomorrow. I've got to write four thousand words about *Sir Gawain and the Green Knight* and if you keep interrupting me every bloody twenty minutes, I'm not going to get it done, am I?'

'How many words are you up to now?'

'Three hundred and fifty-' I counted with my finger, 'seven.'

Jonny pulled a sad face and scratched his finger-nail dolefully against the edge of the door. 'So you don't want to know then?'

I picked up my pen again and looked back down at my essay. 'No thanks.'

'Even though you don't know what it is yet that I was going to say?'

'No.' He was always doing this kind of thing. But I was growing immune to it.

'So you're not interested in the fact that I've been in that shop and had a chat with the bloke who runs it?'

My pen stopped moving. 'Which shop?'

46

'Oh no, if you're not interested, I won't tell you.' Jonny was already out of the room and off down the hallway but I could still hear his voice. 'I mean, you've got to get that *Sir Gawain and the Boring Bollocks* essay written and I don't want to disturb you even if that shop is open and he's giving away all that junk inside. I admire how focussed you...'

'Jonny!' I was up out of my seat and following him into the living room. 'It's *open*? Are you kidding me?'

Jonny shrugged, threw himself into a chair and picked up the TV guide. 'Look, you'd best not go out now anyway. You're right. You *have* got important work to do.'

'Are you kidding!' I picked my coat off the sofa and pulled it on. '*Sir Brain-Drain* can wait. This is much more important. I want to get my hands on that copy of *Fire and Water* before some other bugger does. It's signed, Jonny! I can't risk letting that go.'

Jonny bit his lip and looked at me a little guiltily. 'Are you *sure* you're not too busy? I'm not letting you out of the house if you're too busy.'

'No, I'm fine,' I replied impatiently. 'Are you coming or what?'

It only took us a couple of minutes to walk from our house to the shop. I chatted excitedly to Jonny all the way.

'So what is the guy like who runs the place?'

'Ummm... he's nice. Ginger bloke. Scottish.'

'Did he explain why the shop is always closed?'

'Ummm... he might have done. He had a really strong Glaswegian accent though. I couldn't understand him.'

'And he's just giving – I mean literally giving – stuff

47

away?'

'Uh-huh.'

'All those old music magazines?'

'Uh-huh.'

'Even the records?'

'Guess so.'

'Why?'

'Umm... he says he's emigrating.'

'Really? Where to?'

'Ummm... Jamaica. Yeah, Jamaica.'

'Why?'

'It's where his family come from.'

'Is he Caribbean then?'

'Yeah.'

'But you said he was Scottish.'

'You can have black people from Scotland, you know.'

'But you said he had ginger hair.'

We turned the corner on to Northgate Street. Jonny had gone unusually quiet. I stopped walking and stared at him thunderously. 'Jonny, have you made this all up?'

Jonny bit his lip and gave me a sheepish grin. Unable to speak, I turned my back on him and raced ahead to check that my actions would be justifiable if I throttled him. The shop was locked and bolted. My copy of *Fire and Water* was still gathering dust in the window. I scowled. Engelbert Humperdinck beamed back at me. Jonny's footsteps tapped on the pavement behind me and then stopped.

'You *git*!' I said, rounding on him. 'You made that all up!'

Jonny shuffled from one foot to the other and looked at the pavement. 'It was open earlier, honest.'

'Yeah, right!' I leaned against the glass of the shop-front and folded my arms. 'That was a horrible thing to do. What did you do that for?'

Jonny put his hands on my shoulders. I made no response but I let him keep them there.

'I was worried about you. You've been indoors all day. It can't be good for you.'

'Jonny, I've got to write that essay. *That's* what is good for me.'

He gave me a little smile. 'It can't be that important or you wouldn't have come out at all. I did check that you weren't too busy, remember?'

I sighed heavily, still annoyed.

Jonny stroked my cheek and gave me a slightly bigger and naughtier smile. 'Seeing as you're so close now, we could always go and have a pint in The Coops.'

'*Jonny!*'

'Just a teeny-weeny pint. You won't even notice it and then you can get back to your essay.'

He was grinning now and despite myself, so was I. I followed him into The Coops. The 'teeny-weeny pint' turned into several and then after that it seemed only right that we should go to Rummers for enormous cocktails. My essay was handed in late.

Jonny wasn't the only one to tell stories about that shop at the bottom of Penglais Hill. It seemed that everybody was at it. These stories could be roughly divided into two categories: the friend who'd been in and the friend who hadn't. The latter were usually short tales of woe with little incident that ran along the lines of...

'My friend Aled tried to buy something from that junky music shop the other day.'

'Oh yeah?'

'Couldn't get in though. It was closed.'

The former stories were much more elaborate and were the work of gossips and spin-doctors who had nothing more interesting to do than create themselves a little notoriety by claiming to know someone who had – literally – put a foot in the door. From early on, I suspected that their stories had little of the truth about them. The 'friend' involved was never anybody I could actually track down and the shop-keeper's behaviour and physical appearance changed from one story to the next. One day, I would hear...

'You know Anna who goes around with Helen?'

'No, not really.'

'Well Anna's got this friend called Taz who is big mates with the guy who runs the music shop.'

'What, Andy's?'

'No, the second hand place a few doors down. Well Taz said...'

'Hang on a minute, who is Taz?'

'Taz? I just said. She's a friend of An...'

'How can I get hold of her?'

'Who, Anna?'

'No stupid, *Taz*.'

'I don't know. I think she lives out in Borth or somewhere. But anyway, Taz reckons that Pete, the guy who runs it, used to be the drummer in The Beatles and Pete looks after that place for the owner, *Paul McCartney*. Paul McCartney has a shop *right here* in Aberystwyth. Isn't that cool?'

Another time, I'd hear...

'My mate Elsa was in that record shop the other day.'

'What, Andy's?'

'No the other one. Second hand place. Anyway, the guy who owns it is a right creep. Elsa only wanted to buy the Suzi Quatro album that's been in the window for the last eighty years and the guy behind the counter just kept going on about how he'd love to pierce her belly button for her. What a freak!'

'Who is this Elsa? You've never mentioned her before.'

'Oh she's on my course. Doesn't come out much. You wouldn't know her.'

'The guy who owns it? Did he have a Liverpudlian accent?'

'Hardly. He was Moroccan.'

Once I even heard...

'You know that music shop at the bottom of Penglais Hill?'

'Yeah.'

'Don't go in there, will you.'

'Chance would be a fine thing. It's always closed.'

'Yeah well, just promise me that you won't go in.'

'Why?'

'It's the home of the biggest and darkest coven in the whole of Wales, that's why! If you go in there you're likely to come out again as a bat.'

But even so, I'd have given anything to get on the other side of the front door and have a poke around. Jonny – when he wasn't inventing his own stories to help alleviate his boredom – suggested that I write the owner a note about wanting to buy *Fire and Water* and push it through the door. When I tried to do this, I found that the brass letterbox was so heavy and rusted that I couldn't even open it up enough to get my piece of paper through. Despite the alterations to the window display, the letterbox had not been used for years. Rhys later made the helpful suggestion that I should just set fire to the whole place, wait until the windows had blown out and then calmly take the album out from the display and walk away. Jeremy, who seemed to be the most sensible member of the band but also the most humourless, pointed out that vinyl records should ideally never be exposed to temperatures exceeding 20°C. Rhys snapped, 'I was only joking, *actually*, Jeremy!' I had to intervene and say that I didn't fancy the idea much anyway because I didn't think that I would cope well in prison.

As a consolation, Jonny made me a tape of the album from his own copy and designed his own inlay card with personally tailored sleeve-notes and to-the-second track timings. Each song title came complete with its own special message. But having a tape and having the original on vinyl are not the same thing. And having a *signed* original is another experience altogether.

Donna Karan and Bulldog's conversation has moved on to the notification of impending payments that somebody called Ricky has just received from the Child Support Agency. I am not deliberately listening to them but they are talking so loudly that it is very difficult to avoid hearing. However, I do not have a death wish so I am careful not to make any physical reactions to anything they say. Both women think that the bill is completely unjustified as Ricky was only seeing the child in question's mother for a fortnight or so. Apparently, she had told him she was on the pill. The whole thing was clearly a set up. Either that, says Bulldog, or Ricky has Super Sperm. I've heard as much about Ricky's sperm as I would ever want to so I flick my volume switch back up and listen to some more of Catatonia. Wolverhampton rushes by. I'm glad I'm on this side of the glass.

After Jonny left, the music shop took on a more sinister edge. When he had been with me, it had served merely to tease and frustrate. It tempted me at least twice daily with a prized item that I coveted and offered no explanation of how I might obtain it. But after he had gone, the gentle teasing turned into heartless torment. My album... *our* album... sat public and proud in the window display and reminded me of Jonny each and every time I had the misfortune to walk past. And as I was working up on the campus in the Hugh Owen Library there was little I could do to avoid the shop. Every morning and every evening. Aber is only a little town. It doesn't provide many options in the way of routes around it.

To begin with, I tried staring straight ahead and would not allow myself the painful indulgence of looking in but I found this to be almost impossible to pull off. The torture of walking on up the hill or down further into the town and *wondering* if somebody had finally found a time when the shop was open to buy *my* copy of the Paul Kossoff signed album was too terrible to endure. I *had* to sneak a look. And then when I did and saw my four boys lounging about in all their big-haired and faded glory, I was instantly reminded of Jonny and the fact that he was no longer to be found anywhere in the whole of Aberystwyth. And that realisation would sting me sharply and leave me reeling for a while and then it would give way to a dull ache which I would carry around with me like a heavy load all day or all night and then, just as I was starting to feel a bit better and a bit more positive about things, I would walk past that window again and go through the whole cycle one more time. Day after day after day.

4. Heavy Load

5' 18" Check out the piano.... Sublime.

Finally, three hours and thirteen minutes after pulling out of Aber, I have reached Birmingham New Street. Still carefully avoiding any eye contact with the gruesome twosome, I shove my walkman, book and tapes back into my bag and delve under the seat to retrieve my rucksack. When I look up, I am relieved to see that Donna Karan and Bulldog are already pushing and shoving their way down the aisle. I hang back in my seat for a moment to give them a good lead on me. Borth Woman picks up her bag, gives me another smile and heads off in the opposite direction. I am about to follow her when something catches my eye on the seat opposite. It is Borth Woman's notebook. I haul my rucksack on to my shoulder, grab my bag and snatch up the

55

notebook with my spare hand. More people push their way down the aisle of the train and a wall of bodies divides Borth Woman and me. I stand impatiently and count off the seconds as the man who eats like a hamster pulls his bag out of the overhead rack. I am trapped by him on one side and the Telford Two on the other. The gap between the Borth Woman and me is growing bigger. The man is blocking the entire aisle and packing his things together like a snail. I don't know what to do. Borth Woman is now nearing the end of the carriage. If I knew her name I would shout it out but I don't so I can't and even after sharing the last three hours of my life with her, it doesn't seem right somehow to just shout out 'Hey, Borth Woman! You've forgotten something.'

She is off the train now and heading down the platform; I watch her walk by on the other side of the window. The man who eats like a hamster and moves like a snail is zipping up his hold-all. I take matters into my own hands and push my way past him. He mutters something snide about my manners which is a bit rich really because his apple core is still where he left it on the floor. Still pushing, I make for the door and ignore the grumbles of complaints from all around me. An old lady takes several centuries to manoeuvre her trolley on wheels down the step and over the gap between the train and the platform. I crane my neck above hers and around the door but it is no good. I watch the German army jacket of Borth Woman disappear amongst the crowd. For a second I falter and am unsure of what to do. I look back to see if there is a waste bin that I can dispatch the notebook into but if there is I am unable to see it through the bodies behind me and anyway, the old lady has conquered the gap and I am now being pushed in that direction myself.

As soon as my feet touch the platform, I begin to walk, briskly and automatically. I have made this connection many times before and I know the score. Even with the trains running on time, I am only left with fifteen minutes to make my way across New Street Station to take my train to Ely. If I miss it, I am faced with a longer wait, and even with the shopping centre upstairs, New Street is not really somewhere I want to linger. And anyway, at thirty-one years old, I feel that I have procrastinated long enough.

Upstairs on the main forecourt it is rush hour. Not the wordless and business-like rush-hour of Monday to Friday but the more chaotic and voluminous rush-hour of the weekend coming to life. Serious shoppers are out and about early to bag the summer bargains and their children, too young to be left behind, are screaming toothlessly in their trippers. I look at one who is being wheeled along beside me. He has a crusty nose and a family-sized bag of cheesy puffs in his hand. Tiny bits of orange cheesy puffs are plastered like pebble-dash all over his face. He twists his face upwards and smiles at me. I smile back at him and try to imagine what it would be like to have a little cheesy puff person with me every day of my life. I think I would prefer a rabbit.

Even though it is early, it is already so busy that I am having difficulty walking in a straight line. If I had waited a few hours, I could have avoided all of this and I could have had a cheaper journey into the bargain but it seemed important to me that I should leave Aber on the first train out. Just like Jonny did. Not allowing myself to be distracted by the news-stands and snack bars or by a distant desire to visit the toilet, I walk past the rows and rows of elevators until I come to the head of the one that I need and step aboard with relief. New Street depresses me but I am always careful to remind myself that there is somewhere worse in the world. And that place is Digbeth Coach Station, just a few hundred yards down the road.

By the time I was in my third year, money had become so scarce that I could barely afford to make the journey home to see my family. Realising that I could save a whopping eleven pounds if I travelled by bus rather than by train, I bought myself a bus ticket and subsequently suffered the most horrendous eleven hours of my life. The symmetry of the situation was so perfect it should have been beautiful. One hour of hell for every one pound saved. On reflection, it was a false economy.

And it was Jonny's fault. We'd been to a party the night before and he had encouraged me to get completely incapacitated on pints of snakebite and black. The party was in the house of a flame-haired first-year who called herself MC Curse-Tea and who had quickly gained the reputation of being one of Aber's more serious drinkers. And in a town like Aber, there was no shortage of competition.

'What's with the name?' I'd asked on introduction.

'I'm a DJ,' came the reply as if this were enough. 'You can call me Curse.'

58

Jonny, who was already rather the worse for wear, had barged in at this point, waved a finger accusingly at my new associate and said, 'DJ! Ha! You sit there in your fancy booth playing records but it's people like me who *make* the records. David Bowie or David 'Kid' Jensen? I know whose team I'd rather be on.'

I frowned at Jonny and was about to offer Curse a smile of female solidarity but stopped myself when I saw that she didn't need it. Folding her arms, she put her head on one side, regarded Jonny coolly and said, 'Yeah, well, Mr Big-boy-big-shot, how about I challenge you to a drinking game? Then we'll see what's what. If you win I'll dig your scene but if I win, you dig my scene. Get it?'

I didn't but Jonny must have done because his reply came in an instant.

'Only if my bird can play as well.'

'Jonny! Leave me out of this! I've got to get up early tomorrow.'

Curse grinned. 'Looks like your chick don't cut it, brother. No worries, that leaves more for us.' She linked her arm through Jonny's and, right from under my nose, pulled him off through the crowd. Dumbfounded, I watched as my boyfriend and this other woman departed from my company. Jonny twisted around to look behind him and shouted, 'I'm sure she'll have enough booze for three.' Aggrieved, I pushed my way through the partying bodies and followed them.

We found ourselves in another room. This was somebody's – possibly our hostess's – bedroom but for now it most closely resembled a Nepalese smoking den. A strange creature with several human arms lounged on the single bed and passed a giant-sized spliff from one of its hands to another and then another. Records, ashtrays and empty beer bottles littered the carpet. In one corner, LPs were stacked into a messy tower. I cringed inwardly and knew that Jonny would be cringing too. Anybody with any sense knows that vinyl should always be stored upright. A gigantic yellow and pink poster of De La Soul filled an entire wall. Jonny took in the room, took in the poster and sniffed. 'I hate *dance* music.'

Our DJ friend looked appalled. 'It's not dance music – it's coming-up-from-the-streets Def Jam daisy age hip-hop.'

This revelation was met by two blank faces. Curse shrugged. 'Suit yourself, but if I drink more than you, you've got to promise me that you'll give it a listen.'

Jonny smiled. 'It won't happen.'

Curse walked over to a stereo in the corner, selected a record and put it on her turntable. To the surprise of both of us, the music was not hip-hop at all. It was The Beatles.

'What's your drink?'

'Snake-bite and black,' replied Jonny.

'Me too,' I added, anxious not to be left out.

Curse sat down cross-legged on the carpet, closed her eyes and began shaping her upper body into various tai-chi positions. The many-armed creature on the bed sat up with interest and revealed three heads. Jonny and I looked at each other rather nervously. Eventually, Curse opened her eyes and called, 'Frank, you couldn't line us up some snake-bites, could you? I'm about to have my drinking title contended.'

One of the heads on the bed rose, shouted, 'Hang on a mo', Kirsty,' and scuttled off through the door and in the direction of the kitchen. Curse returned to her tai-chi. Jonny looked at me and winked. Putting his mouth to my ear, he whispered, 'You and me will wipe the floor with this fresher.'

Frank, who we saw now was a girl, returned with several bottles in her arms and a six-pack of lager hanging from her teeth. Offloading her goods, she set three glasses down on the carpet and said to Jonny and me, 'Do you know what you're letting yourself in for? My mate's a champion.'

Jonny shrugged and I yawned.

Frank poured three snake-bites into three glasses, added a splash of blackcurrant and then, as if it were an afterthought, poured a fourth one for herself.

'What are the rules?' asked Jonny.

'It's easy,' answered Frank. 'We're playing 'Help'. Every time you hear the word *help*, you have to drink. Not a girlie sip, mind. It has to be a big manly swig. It's as simple as that.'

Jonny nodded. 'OK, fine. Just one thing. What's the matter with her all of a sudden?' He jerked a thumb at Curse-Tea who was still sat lotus position in front of us. 'Why isn't she speaking?'

Frank looked at us as if we were idiots. 'She's warming up, of course.'

When the record began and the voice of a young John Lennon filled the room, I thought it was going to be easy. For the first few seconds of the song, I thought it *was* easy.

I soon realised that it actually wasn't *quite* so easy – the fizziness of the lager/cider combination was causing uncomfortable eruptions in my nose and the word *help* was coming in such rapid succession that I couldn't make my throat open and close fast enough. By the end of the song, I was too drunk to care.

After that we played a game called 'Roxanne' which was exactly the same principle but using the Police record and after that we played 'Jammin'' using a Bob Marley record and after that, 'My Generation' using one by The Who. After that, MC Curse-Tea told us that she had a problem with blackcurrant, teetered off and threw up in the kitchen sink, dispelling at least twenty-five revellers from that part of the house. The young fresher up-start was taught her lesson and Jonny and I were rapturous in our victory and danced around the bedroom to De La Soul with the girl called Frank and several others who had joined in with the games half-way through.

And all of this would have been fairly standard practice and a perfectly acceptable Friday night's worth of entertainment if I hadn't needed to catch a bus at seven o'clock the next morning.

'You're not travelling very well, are you, *bach*?'

I had only been on the National Express bus for ten minutes. We were barely outside of Aberystwyth. I could have probably walked back to the big ugly house on the end of Llanbadarn Road quite comfortably if I had tried to. In the seat behind mine, an old lady who looked like my Nan was peering through the gap between the headrests and looking at me with eyes full of concern.

'Excuse me,' I mumbled, my jaw wobbling perilously, and – racing against a wave of nausea – I rushed to the loo at the back of the bus.

Curling into a foetal position, I let my jaw hang slack and reacquainted myself with some of the snake-bite from the night before. I stayed, curled up on the floor of the Aberystwyth to Birmingham National Express bus for twenty minutes. Still the bus leaned and lurched along its horrible course. And we hadn't even made it as far as Machynlleth. In that twenty minutes, I was about as intimate with a toilet seat as I would ever want to be. In that twenty minutes, I was sure that I was going to die. There was no way I would ever make it as far as Birmingham and still be alive. I was most certainly going to drown in a miserable pool of my own vomit.

My despair was temporarily distracted by a knock on the door. I squatted, without moving, and hoped the knocker would go away. Whoever it was didn't. Breathing deeply, I rose to my feet, pressed the flush, and opened the door of the toilet. The old lady who looked like my Nan stared back at me.

'You're not travelling very well, are you, *bach*?'

Ashamed and ill, I shook my head.

Through the gap in the door, my new Welsh Nan smiled. My eyes filled up with tears.

'Always been sick, is it? Not used to our roads?'

Again, I shook my head sorrowfully and snivelled pathetically. I liked this old lady. She reminded me of a sweet old woman who once gave me ice-pops when I was a little girl. She reminded me of my own Nanna who I hadn't seen since my parents' separation. Unable to stop myself and not particularly caring anyway, I began to cry.

My Welsh Nan handed me an empty carrier-bag, took hold of my hand and led me back down the bus. 'Dear, dear, dear. We can't have you travelling all the way to Birmingham in the toilet now, can we? No wonder you're feeling ill. That won't help matters. Come and sit next to me and let me look after you.'

I did as I was told and with churning guts and a thumping head, I clutched hold of the open carrier-bag and took a seat in the one behind mine. My new Welsh Nan opened her bag. 'Chew on a couple of these. They'll sort you out. I give them to my grand-children and they never fail.'

She handed me a couple of tiny orange pills and smiled encouragingly as I obeyed her again.

'*Iawn!* Good girl! You'll soon be feeling better and we'll be pulling into Birmingham in no time, just you wait and see.'

I crossed my fingers and hoped that she would be proved right about this one but as the bus went further and the hangover progressed, I didn't get better. In fact, I got a damn sight worse. My temporary Nan told me that she couldn't understand it. Her magic pills had never been known to fail anybody yet! I smiled at her apologetically and resigned myself to the suffering ahead. Pulling my coat over my head and plugging my walkman into my ears, I curled up once more into my favoured foetal position and spent the best part of the journey travelling in darkness with my misery mirrored by the mournful sounds of Leonard Cohen. The other part of the journey was spent back in the loo.

When we at last reached Birmingham, there was some kind of hold-up preventing us from getting into the coach station at Digbeth. The bus was forced to queue in neutral, sending petrol fumes and vibrations in through the open windows. At this point, it finally all got too much. Sick and desperate, I made my way down the aisle of the bus, told the driver that I was on the verge of dying and needed to be let off at once. He started to spout some rubbish about safety hazards and security rules to me but something about my skin tone must have made him change his mind because, not a split-second too soon, he released the door and allowed me to exorcise the last of the snakebite and black on the concrete forecourt of Digbeth Coach Station. All around me, passengers on buses that were headed for all the corners of Britain watched me in my wretchedness. From her position next to the window, the kindly Welsh Nan shook her head at me in disappointment and disapproval. The stain I had left on the concrete was bright blackcurrant purple.

Jonny and I went to loads of parties. He was always invited because he was an Aberystwyth celebrity and I was because he wouldn't have bothered to turn up otherwise. Together, we must have attended more house parties than Noel Edmunds. I suppose that's one of the great things about Aber; in the absence of a bona fide nightlife, people just organise their own.

But after he had gone, the parties began to dry up. At first it was because of the awkwardness thing. Everybody knew that he had moved on and nobody had a clue what to say to me. Conversations with our mutual friends became reduced to 'Hi, how are you? I haven't seen you out for a while. Look I can't chat right now but we must arrange to meet up again later.' Which never happened. Or sometimes, his single male friends would tell me I needed cheering up and promptly ask me out but I was never tempted to take them up on any of these generous offers. I needed time to think.

And what was I thinking about? I was thinking *what the hell am I going to do now?* I hadn't ever considered an Aberystwyth without Jonny in it and the place suddenly seemed to have a very different feel. It had made an uncomfortable shift from being the most beautiful and remote little place in Britain to just being remote. Really fucking remote. But looking on the bright side, I had a job and I had a place to live and I had a handful of friends and the bar staff in Downie's Vaults knew what my 'usual' was. In the end, it just seemed easier to stay.

And when I'd finally stopped thinking and started getting back on with things, I found that there were no party invitations left because everybody I'd known at college had moved on. The people who were now holding the house parties walked past me in the high street and looked straight through me as if I were a local. But they were wrong because what they were seeing, or rather *not* seeing, was just the ghost of a former party-goer.

It is eight thirty and I have made train number two with six minutes to spare. This train is already filling up and I have to walk through several carriages before I spy a seat that is free. It is at a table opposite a suited man who is fiddling with his laptop and looking anxious. I put my things on the table and place my rucksack behind the seat. It is important for me to feel comfortable because this train ride will be almost as long as the last one. The man eyes me unsmilingly through tinted lenses and continues to fiddle away on his ultra-expensive, ultra-fussy keyboard. It is only once I am seated that I look at the items I have placed on the table and remember that I still have Borth Woman's notebook. Filled with sudden curiosity and trepidation, I pick the notebook up and hold it in my hands. I want to know what she has written inside but at the same time, I do not want to do her a disservice. I place the notebook back on the table and drum my fingers up and down on its hard cover. Borth Woman was kind to me earlier and it would be nice to think that her notebook has fallen into safe hands. My fingers drum up and down a little more. It would be nice to think that. But then again, if I look inside I might actually find a name or address so that I can return it to her. In fact, it would be a much better idea all round if I *did* look inside the book. The fingers of my left hand jump to the corners of the cover. I am just about to open the notebook up and take a peak when some inner sense tells me to look out of the window and just at that second, I see the very same Borth Woman taking a seat inside a parallel train inside a parallel universe. My hand freezes and I stare at her open-mouthed. We are completely level with one another and all that separates us are two thicknesses of glass and a concrete platform. I look down sharply. I do not want her to spot me in case she guesses that I am about to pick up her personal notebook and read it. Unable to hold back any longer, I do it.

Borth Woman has been making lists. It seems that I was right about her all along. She has spent far too much time reading Tolkien. From the names scribbled in pencil on the page, I can tell that she has seen the big budget production of *The Lord of the Rings* and now she is secretly planning her own improved version. On one page she has written:

- <u>*Frodo Baggins*</u> *(a hobbit) played by Elijah Wood (film)*
  My choice = Michael Owen (footballer)
- <u>*Gollum*</u> *(hobbit turned evil) animation in film*
  My choice = Rowan Atkinson or Robin Cook (foreign secretary)
- <u>*Gandalf*</u> *(a wizard) played by Ian McKellan (film)*
  My choice = Sven Goran Erikson or Rasputin.

I have to bite my lip to stop myself from laughing out loud. Perhaps my initial impression of her was right after all. She really *is* a nutter. Of all the lists I have ever made in my life, I am proud to say that none of them have been this pointless. I flick through the other pages of her notebook to see if there is anything else of interest but all I see is more scribbled handwriting about hobbits and dragons that I cannot even be bothered to read. I am just about to close the notebook when I notice the edge of another piece of paper poking out from the corner of the book. For the second time in as many minutes, my fingers freeze and then seize on the sheet of paper and pull it free. This new paper is much thicker than the flimsy stuff of the notebook. It is folded neatly into thirds. I unfold it and find myself staring at a letter:

Date: 12 June
Ref: TR1/3458R

WATERMAN, JONES & JASPER
Mrs T E Roberts
Tŷ Lli
High Street
Borth
Aberystwyth

Dear Mrs Roberts

Re: Finalisation of Divorce Proceedings

Your D36 (decree nisi) application has been checked and accepted by the court. I am happy to pass on form D37 (decree absolute) bringing my service to you to a close. The respondent will also be in receipt of form D37 dated as above.

May I take this opportunity to thank you for your kind instructions and wish you every happiness in the future.

If you have any further queries regarding Legal Aid do not hesitate to contact me. I enclose a statement of account showing the balance required from you. Please bear in mind that a personal cheque will require five days to clear.

Yours Sincerely

D Jasper

D E Jasper

The blood has drained from my face and the sheet of paper undulates in my trembling hands. I read the letter again and then look up out of the window. Despite my years of hibernation, I know enough about life to know what this letter means and I know that it is important. The letter's owner is sitting in her parallel train oblivious to my existence. I wave my hand frantically at the window and hope that I can catch her eye. I will show her that I have her things and I will somehow let her know that I will post them on. Mrs T. Roberts – I wonder if she plans to keep that name – is staring out of her window and into space and from where I'm sitting, it seems as if she has the hint of a smile. She has a sweet and carefree face. She doesn't look as if she should be receiving a letter like this. I wave again more urgently but she doesn't move. The man sitting opposite with the tinted lenses and the ultra-fussy laptop gives me a funny look. I seem to be getting a lot of funny looks today. I ignore him and wave again to Mrs Roberts. As I stare, she begins to move away from me. For a second, I am not sure if I am moving backwards or her train is moving forwards. I put my face close to the glass and peer downwards. The platform is still. It is she who is moving on. My eyes fall back on to the letter and it dawns on me that she doesn't want me to send it back to her. She never wants to ever see it again. I am as convinced of this as I have ever been convinced of anything. Screwing the letter into a tight ball, I deposit it and the notebook into a litter-bin behind my seat and wait to move on myself.

Jonny had been gone for six years and seven months and

I'd been going out with Stewart for nearly three months. I picked up my pen.

Dear Stewart,

I raised the pen to my mouth, tapped the end of it anxiously against my teeth, and sat staring at the two words, stark and inadequate on my page.

I know this may come as a shock

Shock? I didn't like that. It was too presumptuous. Who was I to say whether this was going to come as any shock or not? Maybe he wouldn't really care that much at all. Maybe *he'd* be relieved. I took my pen out from between my teeth and placed a line through the word shock.

I know this may come as a surprise to you but I think

Think? This sounded as if I wasn't sure. I was sure.

but I know

Know? Far too harsh.

but I feel that it would be better for both of us

A nice touch. Although of course, I couldn't care less about what was better for both of us. This was purely about what was better for me.

if we didn't see each other anymore

A full-stop here? Perhaps it was a bit too final. I changed the full-stop into a comma and added,

except as friends

That was better. Or was it? To be honest, I didn't really want to be Stewart's friend either. It seemed rather unfair and extreme of me but I was feeling so stifled and trapped by his boring conversations and his boring music and his boring nights out to see boring action films that I really couldn't rule out the possibility that I never wanted to see him again ever. I crossed out the last three words I had written and changed the comma back to a full-stop again. I now had to give him a reason. He'd expect one. That wasn't unreasonable. I'd expect one if I were him.

I feel that we are too different

Too right!

and we don't have enough in common

He might argue that we should *find* things in common. Perish the thought!

and we will never have enough in common to make this relationship

Relationship? God, how serious!

friendship

Too Victorian.

connection

Too Mystic Meg.

to make this meaningless sexual fling

Meaningless sexual fling?

anything more worthwhile. Besides that, I can't stand the way that whenever I'm around your flat, you wash-up everything I touch the very nano-second I've finished with it. What's wrong with leaving things to soak? And why do you turn the edges of the toilet-paper into a point? That's one thing I've never understood about you. The other is why you prefer CDs to records – which I could just about cope with if they weren't such totally crap CDs. Underworld are rubbish and so is Robbie Williams. Despite what you said the other night, Angels is not the best British single ever made. On a scale of how good it is from one to ten, it doesn't even register. And another thing, it really winds me up the way you say 'no pacific reason' all the time and finally, I'd just like to let you know that no, I do not think Chris Moyles is funny. Not even remotely.

I put my pen down, read the letter back to myself and then, with a sigh, crushed the paper into a ball and threw it in the bin.

Stewart wasn't my first failure since Jonny. In those nine long years that I outstayed him, I managed to fail spectacularly with quite a few men. For a while there was Gurt, a Flemish post-grad, who spoke near-perfect English in a perfect monotone. We had near-perfect conversations about perfectly nice things, and Gurt – ever the perfect student – was keen for me to correct him if ever he slipped up with his idiomatic expressions or his phrasal verbs. They say that couples grow alike. I decided enough was enough when I noticed that I was beginning to sound like a Dalek myself.

Then there was Paul. Paul was mostly memorable for being a vegan who weighed less than I did. He stopped me from going into Burger King for a while. BK and I parted company for ten long months. One day, as I was walking down Terrace Road, the temptation must have got just too much. I went inside, sat myself down on a plastic moulded chair and sank my teeth into the most beautiful Bacon Double Cheeseburger I have ever eaten in my life. Paul walked past at the very same moment, somehow caught sight of me inside and promptly dumped me. He said that if we didn't have trust we didn't have anything. I said that if I didn't have a reasonable diet there wouldn't be anything of me left for him anyway. After that, he stormed off and I ordered a BK Flamer with extra large fries and sat in a seat right in the window.

And then there was Ianto. Ianto was the sweetest of that whole bunch of failed boyfriends. He loved rock music and had a huge poster of Reef on his bedroom wall. But lying in his bed and looking at that poster only served to remind me that I was in danger of settling for second best. Reef. Free. It was obvious how they had got their name but Reef were not Free and Ianto was unfortunately too reminiscent of Jonny to be appreciated as an individual in his own right. It hurt to tell him but he needed to be rid of me. He needed someone who didn't have all the excess baggage that I had. So I got shot of him and went out with Stewart. Stewart was nothing like Jonny and had short hair and hated rock music and kept a scrupulously tidy house and thought that Free sounded a bit like a less talented Robbie Williams. Stewart was so dull that he made me want to smoke crack.

Just outside Birmingham, something annoying happens. The train grinds to a halt and rests motionless on the tracks. Everybody sits in silence for the first five minutes or so and then people begin to sigh and mutter and look up and down the aisle as if this will give them some clue as to what is causing the delay. The suited man opposite me glances at his watch every twenty seconds in a manner which would suggest that he suffers from a very acute form of amnesia. All around me, people begin to pick up their mobile phones and fiddle with them but then the speaker system crackles into life.

Ladies and Gentleman, I apologise for the delay. This is

due to a heavy load awaiting clearance in the Nuneaton area. We hope to be moving again within the next ten minutes.

Heavy load? What can this mean? What can be heavier than a diesel engine pulling six carriages packed with commuters and me with my rucksack? Why do they need clearance? Surely, there are people who are paid to arrange this kind of thing. Frustrated and restless, I seek refuge in my walkman and blast my ears with a little bit of The Cult's *She Sells Sanctuary*. But I'm not far into the song when another irritating thing happens. The foot of the suited man opposite brushes against my leg. I sigh inwardly and carefully tuck my feet under my seat so that this intrusion of my personal space barrier will not happen again. I study the man under lidded eyes. He is still tapping away importantly on his laptop and seems unworried by the fact that he has surreptitiously stolen my leg room. Long-legged men like him should be charged more than short-legged women like me. I scowl and close my eyes but within seconds something causes me to re-open them. I have felt his foot again. Without moving my head, I jerk my eyes downwards and see that his left foot is stretched to its full extent under the table and is quite deliberately rubbing against my right calf. My knees bolt upwards and I jar them against the underside of the table. Below the table, the man's foot retracts sharply but above he makes no reaction at all. I bite my nails and am unable to decide what to do next.

The train is still stationary. This adds to my upset. For

some reason, I feel that the problem will only go away once the train starts moving again. I sit, almost in a stupor, not knowing what on earth is going to happen next. Down below me, I glimpse the man's foot move and watch numbly as the tip of his shoe rubs my shin and then begins to travel higher. I look up at him in alarm and although he is still staring fixedly at his computer screen, I see the trace of a smug smile playing on the corners of his mouth. His leg is virtually outstretched horizontally now and his foot is in contact with my thigh. Horrified, I know that I cannot delay taking action for any longer but I really do not know what to do. Nothing like this has ever happened to me before. I take time-out from reality and in my mind's eye, I see myself jump to my feet.

'Excuse me!' I say in a confident and authoritative voice loud enough for people to hear at both ends of the carriage. 'Are you often in the habit of touching women up under the table? Do you do this every time you get on a train?'

The suited man turns green and looks at me in genuine alarm. Everybody else in our carriage has stopped playing with their mobile phones. Across the aisle, somebody giggles. The suited man pulls himself together and recovers enough to shrug.

'You were enjoying it, love.'

He couldn't have said anything worse. I jut my chin in the air and cross my arms. I am aware that he and I hold centre stage and everybody else has forgotten that we are immobile on a train track somewhere between Birmingham and Nuneaton. Fury and fight rise up inside me. I intend to make damn sure that I'm the one who steals the show. I am going to make this train pervert wish he had never been born.

'This man...' I say, turning to the delighted audience, 'This man, ladies and gentleman, is a complete and utter, end to end, up to the ears, signed, sealed and delivered WANKER!'

The crowd break out into applause and jump to their feet. I bask in the glory of a standing ovation whilst the suited man shrivels into a corner.

What *actually* happens is that the suited man's foot is just about to make contact with my crotch when, red-faced, I jump to my feet, dislodging his leg, banging my knees – again – on the table and send his cup of coffee flying. He shakes his head slowly, sighs and mops the coffee up with paper handkerchiefs before it can damage his precious laptop. Somebody across the aisle titters with disapproval at my clumsiness. I grab up my bag and walkman, pull my rucksack out from behind the seat and scuttle off to find another seat in another carriage.

The suited man laughs quietly to himself as I go and the train resumes its journey.

5. Mr Big

5' 55" Raw emotion and torture on the vocal chords – everything that rock should be... and of course the name of the greatest four-piece to grace the bars of Aberystwyth.

Just on the outskirts of Leicester, I start to need the toilet desperately. I twist in my seat and bite my lip because I know that the train is about to stop and I do not want to visit the loos whilst we are waiting at a station. Leicester might look like a toilet to the casual observer but even so, it seems like very bad manners to treat it as one. I chew on my knuckles and hang on in increasing, bladder-splitting discomfort until, thankfully, the train begins to move again. There is a young girl sat next to me; she looks no more than eighteen years old. Her eyeliner is very black and she has piercings in her lip, nose and eyebrow; a few more incisions and she would look like the guy out of *Hellraiser*. I decide to take my bag with me just in case.

The toilet presents a few challenges. There is no lock on the door and to prevent it from swinging open and revealing me at my most inelegant, I am forced to bend forwards and hold the door closed with one hand. However, because I am not very big and my arms are not very long, this means that my bottom barely reaches anywhere near the toilet seat. I am managing remarkably well but then the train hits a rough piece of track and I almost lose my grip on the door. I stumble forward – mid-flow – and end up adding to the puddle of other people's pee on the floor. Not allowing myself to be fazed by this – after all, I've endured infinitely worse at Glastonbury – I wipe my shoes with a bit of toilet paper and selflessly use the other few remaining sheets to clean the floor up a bit. It is only after I have thrown all this down the pan that I discover that the flush does not work. I put the lid down and hope that there will be nobody outside waiting to use the toilet after me.

I am liberal with the amount of soap I take from the dispenser and rub my hands thoroughly. At least something works. Unfortunately, it seems that the soap dispenser is the only thing that does. When I press my foot hard on the floor pump to activate the water tap, not a trickle runs out. The end of the tap is drier than a day out in Durban. I stare at my soap-covered hands for a moment in disbelief and then wipe them on the inside of my coat. Relieved but sticky and smelling strongly of industrial cleanser, I make my way back to my seat.

I discover that during my absence, somebody has jumped into my seat. An enormously overweight man wearing a Marilyn Manson top and sporting the worst haircut I have ever seen in my life is chatting away cheerfully to her out of *Hellraiser*. It's the kind of haircut that suggests he cuts it himself in a darkened mirrorless room using only a pallet knife. I hesitate in the aisle and the pierced girl looks up at me and shrugs and then carries on with her conversation. Feeling almost ready to raise a bit of hell myself, I drag my rucksack out from behind the seat and leave the carriage in search of a third seat on this wretched train.

'Hey, if it isn't Mr Big! Got yourselves a record deal yet?'

Me, Jonny and Waggy stopped what we were doing and turned in unison to see who it was that was calling us from across the street at such an ungodly hour. Spotting the unmistakable blue rinse of the speaker, we all quickly turned back again and pretended that we hadn't heard. The owner of the voice was Martin Hurd – more commonly known by his stage-name Thora – lead singer and chief irritant in The Thora Hurd Experience. Thora cut a striking figure about town. Despite being pale and freckly, he had somehow cultivated an impressive afro after the fashion of his hero Jimi Hendrix which he had then coloured in tones paying homage to his other beloved icon, Thora Hurd. I loathed his hair. Jonny and Waggy loathed all of him.

'What's the matter? Losing your hearing, mate? That might explain some of those dodgy notes you hit the other night.'

Jonny scowled and wallpaper paste dripped off the end of his paintbrush on to the pavement. I took the brush from his hand and whispered, 'Jonny, relax, will you? He's just trying to wind you up.'

'Yeah? Well, it's working.'

Waggy put his brush back into his jam-jar and rolled the remaining posters up. 'Come on. It's time we packed up anyway. The town's waking up. If Plod spots us pasting these fliers up we'll get nicked. And knowing our luck, Thora probably has a direct line set up just so he can grass on us.'

'Hardly. He's up to the same trick.' Jonny gave a sulky nod towards our unwanted satellite who was now making his way across the road and carrying a paintbrush and a bundle of posters similar to our own. To the blue-rinsed man himself, he added, 'What are you shouting at us for? You'll wake the whole street up and get us nicked, you donkey.'

Thora grinned. 'Hey, the publicity might do you lot some good. You need something. The way things are going it looks like you're going to be playing second bill to us forever.'

This time we all scowled. Jonny squared his shoulders and hit back. 'So where's your record deal then? I don't see you lot playing Top of the Pops.'

Thora flushed. 'Maybe not. But we've been played on John Peel.'

Waggy hooted loudly. 'Give a monkey a maraca and he'll get played on John Peel.' He laughed too loudly again and then fell silent. I could tell that despite his mockery, he was impressed. The only radio station that had ever played a demo by Mr Big was one in the Faeroe Islands. And even then, we were all relying on the word of Jeremy's Danish pen friend.

Thora, who had stopped grinning, waved his bundle of flyers in our direction. 'Laugh all you like but this town is only big enough for one band and if you look at all the posters around here, you'll see that The Thora Hurd Experience is right at the top every time.' He stormed off back across the street and disappeared into the early morning darkness.

Jonny spun his paintbrush into the air and then booted it into the gutter with an impressive left-footed strike. 'Gimp!'

'Dickhead!' added Waggy.

I scratched my head and tried to think of something more constructive to say but all I could come up with was, 'You boys really need that top billing.'

And they did need it. Because even though things had been going pretty well for Mr Big throughout the whole of my third year, they were still only the second most popular act in Aberystwyth. That hurt.

Jonny had graduated the previous summer with his expected Third in International Politics and had made the decision to stick around so that he could stay with me but also so he could continue encouraging the vibe which was growing daily around his band. After decades of drought, the time seemed ripe for something to finally happen on the Welsh music scene and with Aber as a creative hub, it stood to reason that one band must surely emerge triumphant.

The only problem was that The Thora Hurd Experience shared not only the same dream but the same bill, and for some reason that none of us could ever understand, they always seemed to come out on top.

Jonny and his band mates worked tirelessly to make sure that if anyone from Aber were about to conquer the world, it would be Mr Big.

The road to fame carried a heavy toll. First of all, Jonny's Mercedes Benz had to go. Surviving only on unemployment benefit, he simply could not afford either the petrol or the insurance. It was a sad day for both of us when he handed over the keys and the logbook to its new owner. Jonny was sad because he prized the car almost as much as he prized his record collection. I was sad because he had promised to drive me up the Cambrian coast to Harlech. To make things even worse, the new owner was none other than Jeremy, the drummer with the secret passion for jazz. Whilst the rest of the band were living on endless cans of baked beans and packets of Smash, Jeremy received occasional cheques from his parents which allowed him to eat reasonably healthily and to purchase the odd luxury item such as a Mercedes Benz when he felt like it. This annoyed Jonny but nobody else was willing to match the two hundred pounds Jeremy was offering. Jeremy promptly painted over all the triangles so it was now an inoffensive pale blue.

But Jeremy played his part too. Although he was not willing to share any of his cheques with the band, he was happy to donate to them the proceeds from his latest business venture *The Gig Machine*. A telephone number was sprayed on the side of the Merc and it was used, not only to transport his own drums around, but also the drum-kits of every other car-less drummer in Aberystwyth. The money he made from this enterprise just about stopped the other three from starving.

Rhys, who played rhythm guitar, was the most inventive of all of them. During the summer months, he juggled blazing paraffin-soaked batons on the seafront, and aside from the occasional singed eyebrow suffered on blustery days, he escaped remarkably unscathed and with an even bigger female entourage in tow.

I don't know why this final detail should have bothered me. There was one time just a few days after Jonny's departure, when Rhys caused quite a stir in my already addled head. I'd been walking along the sea front and had seen him there juggling his burning batons. He had put them down on the ground, given me a petroleum-scented hug and said, 'Jonny's an idiot. I'd never have left you here and pissed off back to Portsmouth.' He had held my face between his hands and added, 'No way!' At that moment, I thought he was going to be another one of those single male friends of Jonny quick to betray him by asking me out. And the funny thing is, if he had, I might well have said yes.

But then he ruined everything by saying, 'I just don't get it. Portsmouth is a shit-hole.'

He probably did me a favour. I'd noticed that he had an unnerving tendency to strike matches and extinguish them in his mouth. He didn't need me to light his fire. He was capable of doing it all by himself.

Publicity was left to me, Waggy and Jonny. We appointed ourselves as the Ministers of Propaganda and sneaked about town at unsociable hours, pasting posters advertising forthcoming Mr Big gigs on lamp-posts and shop-fronts. Even though I found it virtually impossible to drag myself out of bed for a nine o'clock lecture up on the campus, I always managed to join Jonny and Waggy on their dawn-raids on Aberystwyth. We stuck our posters wherever we found a bare space large enough. One time, Jonny slapped a poster on the door of the mysterious music shop at the foot of Penglais Hill and gave me another reason, during the long years that followed, to feel pain whenever I passed.

But even with the cult that they were busily creating around themselves, the prize of a top-billing still eluded them. And maybe, they would never have been offered that coveted slot without my brilliant suggestion. One day as I was walking home from a lecture, I paused again and looked longingly in at the window of the second-hand music shop. On top of a poster advertising a long-since-gone Mr Big gig in The Bay Hotel, somebody had stuck a protest sticker voicing the simple interrogation '*Cymraeg?*' I stared at that sticker for quite some time and then hurried home in excitement. This Welsh language activist had given me an idea that could really turn things around.

I guess it's a case of third time lucky! I have finally found a seat where I feel at home. It's one of those anti-social but altogether more preferable airline-style seats where you have to sit facing nothing worse than the back of the chair in front. And what's even better is that the space next to me is also free so that I can spread myself across the two chairs and discourage anybody from joining me. I make myself comfortable and await the arrival of the trolley service. It's not that I'm particularly hungry or anything. Train journeys put me off my food. If I went on the Trans-Siberia railway I would waste away and die. No, it's just that I've realised I haven't actually spoken to anybody for over four hours. Not even the Telford Two or the Train Pervert in the next carriage managed to get so much as a word out of me. I haven't said anything since I bought my ticket from the man on the early shift at Aber Station. I just want to check that my voice is still working.

Rhys was the only Welsh member of the group and although he couldn't speak Welsh himself, he knew a man who could. That man was called Cefyn. Rhys told us that Cefyn played the French horn for the university orchestra, lived in Borth and studied at the Theological College. Rhys was a pyromaniac who lived in a hovel above a betting shop. How the two had come into each other's acquaintance was a mystery to us all. The day after I had my brilliant idea, Rhys brought Cefyn around our house to meet the band.

'Everyone, this is Cefyn. Cefyn is the man who is going to help us wipe the floor with The Thora Hurd Experience.'

We turned to look at the saviour. He was approximately five feet three and wore rectangular-framed glasses.

The saviour looked back at us, bored. *'Shwmae.'*

Rhys beamed. 'See, I told you he was for real. With Cefyn's help, we'll be able to conquer a whole new market.'

Four faces looked at Cefyn doubtfully. It was Waggy, never one to stay quiet for long, who broke the silence. 'Right, well then, Kev. You know the score. We need you to help us pen a number-one-in-Aberystwyth-chart-busting-smash-hit. In Welsh. Do you think you can do that?'

'*Cefyn,*' said Cefyn, very slowly and deliberately. 'My name's not Kev. It's Cefyn. It's not even spelt the same.'

Waggy who had forgotten his original question, stared at *Cefyn* in surprise for a second. 'Well how's it spelt then?'

'C-E-F-Y-N.'

Clearly confused, Waggy fell silent. Jonny decided to pick up from where Waggy had left off.

'Why?'

This time, Cefyn looked confused. The difference was that his confusion was tinged with a clear dose of irritation too. 'What do you mean, *why?* It's my name. It's how my name is spelt.'

A sly grin slowly spread over Jonny's face. Rhys shifted his feet uncomfortably. Knowing Jonny as he did, he could obviously guess at the jibe which was about to follow.

'So let me get this right,' said Jonny, his brow crumpled into an exaggerated frown, 'You're telling me that your parents liked the name Kevin so much that they gave it the Welshy treatment.' He shook his head in mock amazement. 'Mad! How would they spell Dave then?'

Jonny and Waggy, amidst fits of their own laughter, began to try out various combinations of letters that they thought might answer the question. Cefyn, who by now had turned puce, regarded them ruefully for a moment. 'What's *your* name then?'

90

'Mine? Jonny.'

'I can spell that for you in Welsh if you like,' said Cefyn, still looking furious. 'It's T-W-A-T.'

Jonny's laughter faltered and then vanished altogether.

'Alright, mate. Calm down. I was only having a laugh with you.'

Cefyn looked unimpressed. 'You're the singer, aren't you?'

'Yeah.'

Cefyn smiled for the first time since he'd entered the house. 'So you ought to treat me with nothing less than the deferential respect I deserve, Jonny boy, or I'll put words into your mouth that will make you sound like a right pillock.'

Waggy began to laugh again. This time it was at Jonny. Rhys, Jeremy and I joined him. Cefyn gave a bigger smile. Jonny looked a little nonplussed and turned to Rhys in awe, 'Jesus, your mate's a bit Reggie Kray, isn't he?'

Cefyn, happier now that he had made his point, sat down on the sofa and said, 'Yeah, well, this wasn't my idea. I'm only here because I owe Rhys a favour.'

It was Rhys' turn to look uncomfortable. I reacted to his flush immediately. 'Why is that then, Rhys?'

Rhys coughed and looked at the floor. 'Oh it was nothing, really. Me and Cefyn are just friends from way back.'

'He's teaching me how to tango,' said Cefyn with a wicked gleam in his eye. 'I'm going to join a class but I wanted to know the basic steps before I get let loose on the ladies. Has Rhys never told you he was once Pontypridd's top tango dancer?'

This time we roared. All of us. Even Rhys after a while. And even if he did have any misgivings about his secret dancing past being exposed, he realised that it had at least cleared the air. That afternoon, amid much laughter and the strumming of guitars, Cefyn and the boys thrashed it out amongst themselves and came up with the lyrics and music for Mr Big's greatest ever track. The words were simple – they had to be or else Jonny would never have been able to get his tongue around them. And they were light-hearted. Cefyn quite rightly pointed out that a Welsh audience was not likely to take a long-haired *Sais* from Portsmouth singing in appallingly mispronounced Welsh very seriously. So, after five hours, thirty-two cans of lager and an undisclosed amount of cannabis, Mr Big's break-through Welsh anthem was born... 'Mr Morgan's Organ'. It was a traditional arrangement of verse – chorus – verse with a middle eight thrown in for good measure but like all expertly-crafted pop songs, it was the chorus which was the real hook. Translated into English, it went something like this:

> *He's Mr Morgan*
> *He's got a very big organ*
> *It's name is Ro-land*
> *And he plays it with one hand*
> *That's right, he plays it with only one hand.*

Admittedly, the lyrics were not about to win an Ivor Novello but it became clear that the students, especially the

Welsh-speaking ones, loved them. More importantly, those lyrics got Jonny and the boys invited on to the prized *Slot Pop* on S4C – a three minute filler which allowed unsigned Welsh language bands to make a video and have it aired for the whole of Wales on peak-time television. Looking back with a more objective eye, I suppose that the competition wasn't quite so stiff back then. Apart from a newly-emerged Gwent quartet of disturbed young men in loud shirts and bad mascara, the Welsh rock and pop scene was still pretty much restricted to distant and embarrassed memories of Shaky, the Welsh Elvis, the hero of item number 41 in my childhood rubber collection.

But even this coup came at a cost. What none of us had bargained for was that S4C might actually take Mr Big's efforts to promote Welsh at face value. The letter, on S4C headed paper, should have acted as a warning. It was addressed to Jonny and plopped on to the doormat of the house in Llanbadarn Road, causing much excitement.

'What does it say?' I asked, unable to contain my curiosity.

Jonny frowned. 'I don't know. It's all in Welsh.'

I took the letter from him to check. Since graduating, Jonny had stopped reading – there was a remote possibility that he'd made an unlikely mistake. He hadn't. Jonny and I stared at each other for a moment as the same idea formulated, causing us to shout out in unison: 'Cefyn!'

A quick scramble to find Rhys ensued, which was in turn followed by an even quicker scramble to find Cefyn. We soon found him, less than two hours after opening the letter, in the reading room of the National Library – a place that Rhys, Jonny and I had never previously considered visiting. Cefyn looked swiftly over the letter and said, 'They like your tape. They're sending someone to chat to you next Monday. His name is Owain and he'll have a cameraman with him to help you knock up a quick video.'

It was the news that we all wanted to hear. Cefyn was dragged forcibly out of the National Library and the rest of the day was spent celebrating Mr Big's forthcoming TV debut in the pleasant surroundings of The White Horse.

Five days and nights then crawled by and we wished them away with a slow-burning but persistent impatience. When Monday finally reared its head, Waggy, Rhys and Jeremy arrived at the house early in eager anticipation. Even though I was supposed to be in a lecture, I decided to stick around and give the boys some moral support. I sat with them in the living room and we nervously drank mid-morning sherries and pretended to watch *Richard and Judy* while awaiting the knock at the door.

When it came, it was Jonny who jumped up out of his seat and rushed to open it. The rest of us refilled our glasses, turned off the television and did our best in the intervening seconds to adopt relaxed and casual poses. Jonny reappeared, moments later, trailed by a man who didn't look very much older than any of us and a woman carrying camera equipment. I couldn't help but notice that Jonny looked extremely worried. I frowned. Jonny was rarely troubled by anything. Even a letter he'd had the previous year from the Dean in which he was told that he wouldn't be entered for any final examinations if he didn't start attending seminars, hadn't fazed him. Something was seriously amiss. The man – who had teamed a Tesco employee polo-shirt with a tweed jacket and wore the two with an enviable degree of confidence – smiled, gave the briefest of introductions – 'Owain' – and shook hands with each of us in turn. The camerawoman – dressed more conventionally but sporting plum-coloured hair – followed suit: 'Siân.' On the other side of the room, Jonny was looking increasingly as if he was about to die. Owain and Siân sat down where Jonny had mutely gestured. A notebook was produced and Owain looked up at us all with a big smile. Perplexed, I sat back in my chair and tried to guess what Jonny's problem was.

'*Sut daethoch chi at eich gilydd?*'

A terrified silence descended upon the room. Owain laid down his pen and looked from face to face in surprise and then at Siân, who gave him a puzzled shrug. Behind their backs, Jonny placed his hands on his head and gave a visible cringe. Gingerly, Owain tried again.

'*Ydi popeth yn OK?*'

Jonny's hands slid over his eyes and he silently banged his head against the wall. Rhys, Waggy, Jeremy and I stared mutely at Owain, not daring to turn and look at each other. The same question was reverberating through us all. How could we all have been so totally thick as to expect anything *other* than a Welsh-speaking interviewer? Finally, it was Rhys who spoke up in a very small and apologetic voice.

'I'm really sorry. We don't understand Welsh.'

'Oh, right.' Owain's surprise seemed to be growing by the second. 'I'm sorry, I just assumed – what with the tape and the nature of the programme and everything.' He closed his notebook and thoughtfully drummed his fingers on its cover. 'I'm not sure how we stand now.'

'How d'you mean?' asked Waggy, finding his tongue. 'It doesn't make any difference. We can still perform 'Mr Morgan's Organ' with no trouble. Jonny's spent ages learning the words to that.'

Owain shook his head. 'No, it's not that. I know you can perform the song, I've heard the tape, remember? It's just that this will have an impact on the funding we receive to make this programme. The idea was that we use *Slot Pop* to promote Welsh language bands.'

'But 'Mr Morgan's Organ' *is* Welsh language.' Waggy had an idea of the way this conversation could be heading and he was not about to let his opportunity to appear on prime-time TV disappear without a struggle.

Owain sighed. 'That one song is, certainly. But Mr Big are not. And I was led to believe that you are. We can't go ahead and make the video without at least one of you being a Welsh speaker because otherwise that would open the floodgates for lots of cash-in videos of token Welsh songs and that's not really the point of the programme.'

'Well, Rhys speaks a bit of Welsh, don't you?' said Waggy a little desperately.

Owain looked at Rhys. *'O, wyt ti?'*

Rhys gulped nervously. *'Dwi'n hoffi coffi.'*

Owain and Siân looked at Rhys blankly for a second and then roared with laughter. Rhys turned the colour of his flaming batons and scowled sideways at Waggy.

'What did you say?' asked Waggy.

'He said he liked coffee,' said Owain as he began to pack his notebook away. 'And whilst that is interesting I'm not sure that the answer was entirely relevant to the question I asked. I'm sorry, I really am. I admire the trouble you've gone to and I would really like to give you a break but we'll be in trouble with our bosses if we change the rules now.' He stood up. I looked across the room at Jonny who had by now taken his hands away from his eyes. Our eyes met, and once again, the same idea crystallised: *'Cefyn!'*

Owain turned to Jonny. 'What?'

Jonny closed the door of the living room and positioned himself in front of it, cutting off our visitors' escape. 'We *have* got a Welsh-speaking member of the band – it's just that he's not here because he's a lazy git and he's probably asleep somewhere. Rhys, go and find him.' Cottoning on quickly, Rhys did as he was told and fled from the room, promising to be no longer than twenty minutes.

'And what instrument does this Kev play?' asked Owain, looking at his watch.

'Not Kev! *Cefyn!*'

Owain sat back down startled. We hadn't meant to shout at him.

'C-E-F-Y-N,' I added helpfully.

'And he plays the French horn,' said Jonny.

'The French horn?' Owain was starting to look a bit alarmed. I think we were frightening him. 'In a rock band?'

Jonny flushed and faltered so Jeremy, who up till now had wisely stayed silent, took over. 'It gives us an unusual quirky brass element that most rock bands don't have.

We're kind of Creedence Clearwater Revival meets the London Philharmonic.'

Owain and Siân looked at each other with raised eyebrows. The rest of us held our breath. It was Siân who spoke first. She shrugged her shoulders, gave a smile and effortlessly granted Mr Big a reprieve by saying, 'Well, let's wait for this Cefyn, shall we? I'm finding this band more and more intriguing.'

When Rhys eventually returned with Cefyn in tow and Owain and Siân had satisfied themselves as to his Welsh language credentials, Cefyn was silently drafted in as Mr Big's newest addition – the French horn player. It seemed like a good idea at the time. We all walked down to the ruins of the castle and Siân filmed the boys pretending to play their instruments in the wind and rain. Jonny had borrowed a Roland keyboard from Tristan and the Killer Toasters and he added an extra X-rated dimension to the proceedings by pretending to make love to it.

When we saw the video which appeared on TV three weeks later, I couldn't help secretly thinking that Siân had been so adventurous with her camera angles that the whole thing made me rather sick to watch. At some points, the close-ups were so extreme that I could see all of Jonny's fillings whilst he was singing. And the long lingering shots of Rhys' thrusting crotch struck me as not entirely necessary – many people would be eating their tea at the time of transmission, after all. But Jonny and the boys loved it. Mr Big were on the lips of every student in Aberystwyth and Jonny suddenly found himself shadowed by a whole new group of girls who shouted at him in a language he couldn't understand. More importantly, Mr Big's TV appearance rewarded them with the prize they had coveted for so long and that prize came in the form of the annual Up Top Rock Night. The Up Top Rock Night was one of the biggest dates in the Student Union's calendar and anyone who was anyone – in Aberystwyth – was going to be there. Anticipation and excitement about the gig was at fever pitch. We all knew that this could be the big one. Especially as it had leaked out that not one but *two* record company scouts had already accepted invitations to attend.

There were only three slots on the bill and competition was fierce. It was widely known that the Student Union stalwarts Not The Comfy Chair had lost out on being the show's opener to a relatively unknown but highly touted bunch of young upstarts called Heavysidz. But more important and less certain was the matter of who would close the gig. Up until the S4C airing of 'Mr Morgan's Organ' it seemed that the union entertainment's manager would follow previous form and give the top billing to The Thora Hurd Experience. But after that seminal three minutes, he changed his mind....

The 'Up Top Rock' Night

Presents

MR BIG

The

Thora
Hurd
Experience

&

Heavysidz

Tickets £5 – Union & Neville's Boutique

The name of Mr Big moved up to the highest echelons of Aber showbiz society and The Thora Hurd Experience were humbled. Mr Big were on their way.

I come to life with a violent start. My head is thick and heavy and something about the tastes and textures inside my mouth makes me feel as if I have spent the past ten years licking a snooker table. For a split-second, I'm not even sure where I am but then the tell-tale tremor kicks back into gear and reality descends upon me once more. I stretch in my seat and rub my eyes, covering my knuckles with mascara in the process. I sigh and wipe my knuckles over my jeans but the mascara sticks so I then try to inconspicuously lick the mascara off. My mouth is so dry that my tongue threatens to stick to my hand. Across the aisle I can see a woman with a cup of something hot in front of her. She has one leg crossed over her knee and is swinging her foot a little as she sips her drink. I can't help noticing that she is wearing a very classy pair of blue and yellow trainers that I have never seen on anyone else before. This woman really seems to have it all. My eyes flit enviously from her trainers to her drink and then back again. I want those trainers. I add them to a list in my head entitled *Things I Want but Can't Have*. My eyes switch back to the drink. This is something I *can* manage. I turn to my bag and am about to look for my purse and go in search of the refreshment trolley when another thought stops me in my tracks. This thought is big. And stressful. I forget all about my need for a drink.

I don't know where I am.

I know that I am on a train of course but beyond that I have absolutely no idea where in Britain I am. I sit rigid in my seat and fight the searing flames of panic inside me. The last thing that I can remember is being on the eastern side of Leicester and waiting for the refreshment trolley to come and now it seems that the trolley has been and gone and I don't know when it came exactly or where on earth I am now. Obviously, I am somewhere in Eastern England but – forgive me for being a stickler for detail – I need a little more accuracy than that to calm me down. Right now, I need to know where I stand. Or sit.

Outside, the land is flying past, endless and flat. I can see for miles and miles and miles. Unfortunately, I cannot see any signposts. Maybe I am in Kansas. I take another look at the expanse of bland boggy greyness rushing by me and dispel the idea. I have seen *Little House on the Prairie* and I know that Kansas looks nothing like this. The Ingalls family would have packed-up their gear and headed for the Big Apple if they had been confronted by these views every morning.

No, I am familiar with this journey and I know exactly where I am... roughly. I am in Cambridgeshire. The thing I need to know is if I am north or south of Ely because that is where I have to get off to make my connection and this train is going on as far as Cambridge; a nice city rightly enough but somewhere I don't want to be. I sit back in my seat, breathe in and out slowly a few times and consider my options. I could ask Cool Trainers if we have been through Ely yet but I am not keen to do this. The simple reason for my reluctance to put this plan into action is that if she says yes then not only will I feel like a fool but she will know that I most definitely am one.

The other option is to do nothing; to sit tight until the train makes its next stop and then take things as they come. Except that I am now in such a state of agitation that I could not sit still if my life depended upon it. If I have missed my stop it will add at *least* another hour to my journey time and that one unnecessary hour could just be the one to push me over the edge. I could lose my entire mind in that hour. I could be riding the trains of Eastern England forever. Benevolent passengers would keep me alive with sandwich crusts and the dregs from their polystyrene coffee cups. I'd probably even grow a beard. Train-spotters from all over Britain would come here deliberately just to try and catch sight of me.

I stare blankly into space for a moment and then the vaguest hope of a solution begins to form in my head. It is an old game I used to play as a student to occupy my mind on this flat and viewless stage of the journey. I twist in my seat and scan the horizon to my left. I can see marshland and the occasional twisted tree and a few slow moving cars and a larger, more promising stationary dot on the landscape. I squint harder and stare at it some more but then it begins to move and I guess that it must have just been a lorry or some other large vehicle making a delivery to the embattled people who live in these parts.

Completely absorbed now, I rise, move into the aisle and stare out of the right side window. Again, I scan the horizon like a hawk and search for any solid stationary blot on the landscape. Miles and miles of marshland surround me. I am almost about to give up and accept the worst when my eyes seize on something. It is no more than a speck. I can blot it out entirely with the nail of my little finger. It is dark and still but becoming a little larger and more solid. I keep my eyes fixed on to it and hope. Some sixth sense tells me that Cool Trainers has stopped swinging and I can guess that its owner is watching me and wondering what I am up to but I do not allow myself to be distracted. I have to focus all of my attention on the blob on the horizon. If I take my eyes away, even for a second, I will lose it. The train rushes on and on and still the blob is there and I can see it growing. After a few minutes, I even believe that I can make out the ragged edges of tiny spires and flying buttresses. Satisfied, I breathe a deep sigh of relief, smile to myself and return to my seat. I have not missed Ely. From my expert judgement calculated by the size of the blob, I would say that I am some fifteen minutes north-west of Ely Cathedral. Panic over.

Back in my seat, it suddenly strikes me that another option would have been to look at my watch and then consult my timetable. But that would have been far too sensible.

After everything was said and done and Jonny had recovered enough to lick his wounds and allow himself to reflect, he simply said that the timing was all bad. 'Of all the days in all the years of all my life,' he said, 'to learn that I can no longer call my band Mr Big because a bunch of permed soft-rockers from Hicksville have beaten me to it and got into the Top Ten with some mushy love song that everyone hates, *that* day had to be the worst. Why the hell did it have to be the morning before our biggest ever gig?' Put like that, he was right. The timing was all bad. Shockingly bad.

We all followed the charts pretty closely in those days because, even with the arrival of Kylie and Jason, they were still worth following. Even the stuff we didn't like at least had some sort of creativity about it; it wasn't all pop svengalis and stage school kids back then. On the morning before the gig, Jonny and I had sat in the living room breakfasting on coffee and roll-ups and watched *The Chart Show* as we always did. Most of the programme was dominated by laughable pap sung badly by Australian soap stars but it was the number three slot of the network chart which stunned us both into silence. *To Be With You* was a softly-sung ballad by a Los Angeles rock band we had never heard of before. They were called Mr Big. To be honest, I quite liked the song but Jonny was appalled. He stared open-mouthed at the television. 'They can't call themselves that; it's our name.'

I tried to be reasonable. 'I don't suppose they realised that, Jonny. I know it's shocking but they've probably never been to Aberystwyth and heard you play. Come to think of it, they've probably never heard of Wales either.'

Jonny could not be consoled. He phoned the other members of the band and summoned them to the house for a council of war.

I didn't really see what all the fuss was about; surely the world was big enough for two bands called Mr Big, especially as one band didn't even have a recording contract or any fans outside Aberystwyth. But Jonny didn't see it that way. Jonny said that any record company scouts turning up to the gig that night would just laugh at a band who had the same name as a current top ten act. He said it would be just like calling themselves The Stone Roses. Looking back now, I think that Jonny was wrong to compare Manchester's Stone Roses with LA's Mr Big but that's just another item in a great long list of things that I never got to tell him.

So the boys sat and thrashed it out and tried to come up with another name. The discussion was supposed to be civilised. It wasn't. I retired to the kitchen to make tropical flapjacks and kept myself out of the way but I could hear everything that was said because they were shouting at each other. Cefyn started it by suggesting that they just opt for the Welsh and call themselves Mr Mawr but Waggy got all upset and said there was no way he was going to be a part of any band that he couldn't even pronounce properly. Cefyn responded by calling Waggy a fascist. Then Jeremy announced that he wanted to call the band J's Rhythm Quartet but everyone else protested.

'J's Rhythm Quartet,' snarled Rhys, louder than the others. 'As in J for Jeremy? Who do you think you are? You're only the bleeding drummer.'

Through the open door, I saw Jeremy turn purple and scowl at Rhys. 'Fuck off! If it wasn't for my drumming, you and your guitar wouldn't even be on the same song as the rest of us. Your time-keeping is shit. You're such a –'

We never got to hear what Rhys was because Jeremy wasn't given the chance to finish.

'We are most certainly NOT going to be called J's Rhythm Quartet because we're a *quintet* now if you hadn't noticed.' The interruption was from Cefyn who had not been invited to the day's proceedings but who had somehow got wind of them and turned up anyway. 'What about Mr Mawr Quintet?'

'I still can't fucking pronounce it!' shouted Waggy. 'And anyway, who are you to make a suggestion? You're not really in this band. You've just been tagging around us ever since those S4C people came down. We don't need a bloody French Horn player.'

'Oh don't you?' Cefyn sounded as if he was either about to explode or implode. 'That's funny. You needed me the other day. I'm part of this band now and you better get used to it because you'll be learning to play my songs soon.'

'*What?*' The roar unmistakably originated from Jonny. '*I* write the songs. I always have done and I always will. 'Mr Morgan's Organ' was a one-off.'

'Oh was it?' Cefyn's voice had reached a screech. I peered around the door and checked to see that he was still all in one piece. He was. 'I wonder what your new army of fans would think about that? I wonder if they know it's just a bloody novelty record?'

Jonny seemed about to yell back but then hesitated and instead muttered, 'Reggie Kray!'

Cefyn gave a chilly smile. 'So we're agreed on Mr Mawr Quintet then?'

'No we're fucking not!' If Jonny was willing to make concessions, this wasn't one of them. 'We're not being called

Mr *anything* quintet. Or quartet. Or trio. It sounds like a poxy jazz name. We're not jazz. We're rock, remember?'

At this point, there was a commotion, the kitchen door flew open and I was joined by Jeremy who had stormed out of the discussion in a sulk. For a while, it looked as if the group might disband before the gig was even played. It was Waggy who managed to provide a breakthrough.

'I know what Jonny means,' he said through clouds of blue smoke. 'We're a rock band so we've got to sound like a rock band. It's all about who we are. I feel like I'm a member of a band called Mr Big and I don't want to turn around and be a member of something else. Do you see what I mean?'

Jonny nodded triumphantly and Jeremy stood in the doorway of the kitchen and shrugged. Cefyn mulled the question over in his head and then asked, 'Am I in this rock band?'

Waggy sighed, 'Guess so.'

'Fine.'

Rhys had a lighted match inside his mouth so he didn't say anything.

'And anyway,' continued Waggy, who had suddenly discovered the voice of reason and was enjoying using it. 'Loads of brilliant bands have had the word *Big* in their names... Big Audio Dynamite... Big Brother and the Holding Company... Big Country.'

'Big Fun,' added Jeremy from the doorway, still sour.

Waggy tactfully chose to ignore the interruption. 'So why don't we just call ourselves something along the same lines as before. Like The Real Mr Big Band.'

'Too jazz!' interrupted Jonny who either had a bee in his bonnet about this issue or was just deliberately winding Jeremy up.

'Or The Mr Big Membership or some other compromise?' Waggy was not about to let Jonny destroy the cease-fire so easily.

Jonny scratched his head. 'Big Membership is too much of a mouthful.'

'Well what about Big Member then?'

The room filled with silence. I left my flapjacks again and checked that the boys were still alive. A grin appeared on Jonny's face. It was the first time he had smiled in two hours. He stood up and began pacing. '*Big Member*. I like it. The audience will know that we're members of Mr Big but they'll also know that we've got the – ahem! – dimensions to live up to the name. Who agrees on Big Member then?'

Waggy and Rhys raised their hands. Jeremy, still standing in the doorway of the kitchen said, 'It's shit!' Cefyn decided that he was abstaining.

'Big Member it is, then,' said Jonny looking pleased. 'Now *that* is a real rock name.' He grabbed his crotch in a victorious salute and the matter was settled.

The train pulls into Ely station twenty minutes late but it doesn't matter because I still have an hour and a half to wait for my next connection. Cool Trainers gets off as well. She is met on the platform by a dark-haired sexy man who rushes up to her and gives her a big snog right then and there for the whole world to see. I walk past them and buy myself an ice-pop in a café called The Lemon Tree. The mute and surly woman who takes my money looks at my purchase as if I have made an odd choice. I don't care. I have always loved ice-pops. Walking outside, I take a seat on the platform. From where I am I have a good view of the station car park and I can see Cool Trainers and her sexy man getting into a natty little vintage MG. I watch them until I can no longer see them and then give a small sigh of relief. I am glad Cool Trainers and I are no longer sharing each other's worlds. That woman was beginning to make me feel inadequate.

I sit on the bench and look around for something else to think about and my gaze falls on the sign of the café. The Lemon Tree is not a good name for a café on a platform on a train station in Ely. I can't see a single tree from where I'm sitting and experience tells me that I'll see precious few either during this stretch of the journey. In this part of the world, it's all grey sky and peat bogs and the occasional teenager on Prozac. Not many trees. And not that many lemons, either.

Everything was ready to go. The set had been rehearsed. Jonny's hair had been washed. Cefyn had been fully briefed on exactly where and when he was allowed to add a little French Horn accompaniment and the posters and flyers had been cunningly doctored with the aid of a pot of glue and some paper.

The 'Up Top Rock' Night

Presents

MR BIG Member

The

Thora
Hurd
Experience

&

Heavysidz

Tickets £5 – Union & Neville's Boutique

Jonny, Rhys, Waggy and Cefyn put on their best clothes and walked with me and their instruments up the hill to the Union. Jeremy drove himself and his drum-kit in the Mercedes Benz. Apparently, there wasn't room for anyone else. At the top, I watched the boys do their sound-check and then left them to it whilst they settled themselves comfortably into the kitchen of the Union Pizza Bar which was doubling up on this auspicious occasion as back-stage. I wandered off to find other entertainment. I knew better than to bother with Jonny and the boys before a gig. Afterwards was fine because they were always happy and excited and floating on a natural high but beforehand there could well be tension and I preferred not to be a part of it. Jonny never drank immediately before a gig; he said that it compromised his professionalism. It was the only time I could guarantee that I would always be able to find him sober and I respected him for that but preferred to stay out of his way until afterwards when he would drink again.

Back among those that Jonny called *the punters*, the atmosphere was reaching a state of frenzy. The hall looked full to capacity and the opening band were already coming close to the end of their set. The new kids, Heavysidz, were going down a storm. Close to the stage, I spotted my long-forgotten friend Kate and pushed my way through the throng to join her up the front for a bit of serious moshing. Clearly Kate's aversion to paying entrance fees to gigs was less acute nowadays. She greeted me with a wave and an easy grin – a mosh pit was no place to bare old grudges, after all. I could feel a bonding vibe down there that was positively primeval. We were rocking. Heavysidz were rocking. Jonny could not have hoped for a better warm-up act. The lead singer – a flame-haired girl who had a stage presence somewhere between Janis Joplin and Johnny Rotten – growled her way to the end of another song and paused to take a big swig from a bottle of Thunderbird positioned just next to her mic stand. I caught her eye and a memory was triggered. I turned to Kate and yelled, 'I've seen her before somewhere. What's her name?'

Kate shouted a name back at me but it was lost, because the drums and bass had already begun again. The singer put her lips to the mic and snarled, 'THANK YOU ABERYSTWYTH AND FUUUUUCCCCK OFFFF!'

The crowd roared.

'This is the last one and it's called *Teenage Angst*.'

The music was loud and the words were easy. After we had heard them once, we all joined in.

> *Don't talk to me about school*
> *Don't need no Bunsen Burner*
> *I'm a special needs learner*
> *Don't talk to me about maths*
> *If there's one thing makes me weary*
> *It's Pythagoras' fucking theory*
> *Don't talk to me about God*
> *Samson and Delilah*
> *What a massive pile o'*
> *Shit shit shit*
> *Shit shit shit*
> *Shit shit shit*
> (repeat until fade)

We did.

After Heavysidz had finished their set, there was a fifteen minute interlude whilst The Thora Hurd Experience carried their equipment on to the stage to a backing track of the similarly named but much more commercially successful (and musically talented) Jimi Hendrix Experience. Worn out by my exertions, I stationed myself at the bar and ordered a pint of snakebite and black. Unlike Jonny, I had absolutely no qualms about drinking prior to one of his gigs. In fact, most of the time I usually drank for the two of us.

Just as The Thora Hurd Experience were breaking into the opening chords of their tried and tested crowd-pleaser *Poxy Lady*, I found myself joined at the bar by none other than the school-hating angst-ridden singer of Heavysidz. She ordered herself a pint of scrumpy, downed it in one and then requested another. I watched, impressed. She repeated the same trick all over again and then turned to me and said, 'You're the girlfriend of that bloke from Mr Big, aren't you?'

I nodded, quietly pleased to be recognised but thought I ought to put her straight about the name change. 'They're called Big Member now, on account of those guys in the Top Ten.'

My companion took a thoughtful swig and downed another third of her third pint.

'Big Member? Cool.' She nodded her head thoughtfully and then after placing her glass back on the bar, started making some tai-chi motions with her hands. A fleeting firework of déja-vu exploded in my head. I definitely knew this girl from somewhere. I decided to clear the matter up. 'Don't I know you?'

'I don't know, *do* you? I can tell you one thing; I don't hang out with no rock star boyfriend like you. My name's Curse-Tea.'

If there was any trace of sarcasm earlier in her answer, my brain skimmed over it and seized upon her last words. 'Curse-Tea! I *have* met you before. At a party in your house last year. I thought you were a DJ, not a rock chick.'

Curse-Tea abandoned her tai-chi and turned to me. 'I was. But I dropped that. The deal was that if I lost the drinking game I'd listen to a bit of rock music. Don't you remember that?'

I shook my head. I didn't generally retain any of the finer details about the parties I attended.

'So I lost the game and got listening to all of this rock stuff. Then I decided that your fella was right. David Bowie *is* a cooler team captain than David 'Kid' Jensen, so I switched teams and started my own band.' I stared at her confused. I really had no idea what she was talking about. Curse-Tea took another mammoth mouthful of scrumpy – there seemed to be no danger of her ever losing a drinking game again. 'So really, in a round-about kind of way, it's your bloke I have to thank for being the brainchild of Heavysidz. Don't you see?'

I nodded but I was not sure that I did.

'So what do *you* do?'

The question took me by surprise. 'What?'

'*I'm* in a band. Your *Jonny's* in a band. *Everyone* I ever see you with is in a band. What do *you* do? Do you play

115

anything?'

I drank some of my snakebite to buy myself time. Reaching the bottom of the glass, I plumped for Pamela Morrison's preferred job description. It hadn't done her any harm, unless you counted her heroin-related death a few years after Jim's.

'I'm the ornament.'

Clearly Curse-Tea liked my answer. She roared with laughter, clapped me on the back and shouted, 'Barman, give us another couple of chasers.' The barman, who seemed a bit frightened, did as he was told. Curse-Tea downed the rest of her third pint. 'Well, you may be on your way to becoming a very expensive ornament because your fella and his mates are good. Everyone reckons those cats are gonna get signed tonight.'

Cats? My eyebrows shot up and I eyed her suspiciously but she seemed to be serious. Maybe this was the way that people with names like Curse-Tea spoke.

'I hope so,' I said and smiled.

Curse-Tea leaned over as if to tell me something in confidence but the noise now being generated by Thora and his mates meant that she actually had to bellow loudly in my ear.

'They're here you know, these record company people. Keep your eye out for a couple of dads. They both look at least thirty. One of them's got a pony-tail and the other one is a bit of a receder. But they're the ones you want to watch. It's survival of the fittest. Your boy has got to make an impression tonight. I'm rooting for him.' She took a first swig of her *fourth* pint and then, fixing her mouth to my ear again, adopted an even more confessional tone. 'I may as well root for him because there's no way *my* lot are ever going to get a record deal.'

For a moment, Curse-Tea's shoulders drooped and the energy and vitality I had seen on the stage just a short while before seemed to belong to another individual altogether. I searched for some words to revive her spirit.

'Hey, I thought you were great. The crowd thought you were great. What's the problem with your band?'

Curse-Tea rolled her eyes and pulled a face. 'Wankers. Too many wankers in one room at any one time and too much in-fighting. People think we're good but it's me who's good; the rest of them are shambolic. To get myself noticed, I need to get me a band like your fella's. They've got a more professional approach.'

With that she drank some more of her drink, regained her grin and suddenly broke out in a rousing chorus of Big Member to the tune of Shirley Bassey's *Big Spender*. I joined in and then summoned over the barman who eyed my drinking partner warily.

'Can I get you a drink, Curse?'

'Want to share a bottle of Thunderbird?'

'Do they sell that stuff behind the bar?'

Curse-Tea winked. 'They do for me – it's on my rider. How about it?'

'OK then, why not?'

If I'd been a little more sober I'd have been able to answer the question myself. The reasons *why not* were obvious. Firstly, I knew that mixing my drinks was a disastrous move which would leave me feeling like the arse-end of a monkey's armpit when I woke up the next morning. Secondly, Thunderbird tasted like shit and was drunk by dossers. These were reasons enough. Nevertheless, I accepted the offer and me and my new friend drank our way through the entire bottle and sang our new anthem as loudly as we could in a vain attempt to drown out Thora as he thundered his way through *All Along the Glengower* and *Crosskeys Traffic*.

> *Hey Big Memberrrrr*
> *Spend a little time with me.*
> *So you want to have*
> *Fun*
> *Fun*
> *Fun....*

Things were a bit foggy for me by the time that Jonny came on to do his set. I sat on my high stool and gripped on to the bar for safety as my beautiful boy swaggered on to the stage and took up his position at the microphone. He cleared his throat and I held my breath.

'Thanks to those tossers in the charts, we shall from now on be known as Big Member.'

There were a few ripples of laughter from the crowd. Jonny scowled. He didn't like being laughed at. For a moment, I feared that he might retaliate and engage the crowd in a slanging match but Rhys saved him by quickly breaking out into the opening chords of their opening tune – the familiar and mighty sound of *Sex for Breakfast*. The crowd was appeased and I breathed a sigh of relief. By the time the boys had finished their second track – *Latvian Lovers (Have Cold Flats)* – the crowd were back in their rightful adoring place. I bopped up and down on my stool and yelled out for more. This gig was really rocking.

But unfortunately there wasn't more. Just as Jonny was singing the opening lines to *Takes A Freak To Know A Freak*, the microphone was snatched from him and the backing music came to a faltering stop. Some fool from the crowd had embarked upon a single-handed stage invasion. Agitated, I raised myself up on my barstool so as to see better what was happening. A feisty flame-headed hippy had wrestled the microphone from his hands and was standing blinking in the glare of the lights, momentarily unsure of quite what to do next. The crowd hushed in both confusion and anticipation. The stage-invader, realising that some further action was immediately required, raised the microphone to her lips, grinned broadly and then began to sing at the very top of her very powerful voice.

Hey Big Memberrrr
Spend a little time with me.

Appearing to have forgotten how much they had been enjoying Big Member's set just a moment before, the crowd joined in enthusiastically. The girl on the stage was now busy throwing various items of her clothing into the delighted crowd. Battling against a rising tide of jaw-numbing sickness, I turned to my left. My friend, Curse-Tea, had disappeared.

By the time I could comprehend what had happened,

119

I was certain of two things. One, Jonny would be furious if he ever found out that I had accompanied this girl in getting so very drunk and two, Jonny was going to be furious anyway. Really very seriously furious indeed.

It took the bouncers about ten minutes to get Curse-Tea off the stage. But by the time that she was restrained, it was all too late anyway. Enraged at being upstaged, Jonny and Waggy had tried to manhandle her off the stage themselves before the bouncers had arrived, prompting various other members of the Heavysidz entourage to storm the stage in protest and embark upon a full-on fist fight. Somehow in the confusion that followed, Jeremy managed to land a punch square on Jonny's nose causing him to instantly lose some of his prettiness forever. In response, Jonny suddenly forgot about the ongoing battle with Heavysidz and decided he'd rather beat-up Jeremy instead. The job of defending the pride of Big Member was then left to Rhys and Waggy alone. Cefyn opted instead to make the most of this golden opportunity and seize the limelight for himself by providing a haunting solo French horn soundtrack to the increasingly lively events on stage.

Meanwhile, Curse-Tea, the cause of the riot, must have been feeling the less pleasant effects of her four pints of scrumpy and half bottle of Thunderbird. Frozen to my seat at the bar, I watched in ever-growing horror as she staggered away unnoticed to the corner of the stage and threw-up spectacularly over several thousand pounds worth of amplifier equipment. The Union plunged into darkness and screams overwhelmed the plaintive notes of Cefyn's horn playing.

'What's happened?' I shouted to the barman.

'Your crazy mate has short-circuited our electricity supply.'

'Oh crikey!' I really couldn't think of anything else to say. Jonny was going to be furious.

Student Union officials marshalled everybody out of the building as quickly as they could, and all the way down Penglais Hill students walked home, already preparing their letters asking for their money back. Rhys, Waggy, Jeremy and Cefyn were driven down in a big black police van they were forced to share with Heavysidz. Jonny, whose nose was now bleeding heavily, got his ride down the hill in the back of an ambulance. His only souvenir of his first ever headlining gig was to be a broken nose and a severely dented ego.

The A n' R men, who had come to see the light and discovered only mayhem, left as discreetly as they had arrived.

Up Top Flop!

Graham Tomlinson, Arts and Media Correspondent, reviews another night of musical mayhem at Up Top Rock.

WHEN Martin 'Thora' Hurd took to the stage last Saturday night and chose to greet his fans with the words, 'Hey Joe, where are you going with that leek in your hand?' the assembled crowd at Up Top Rock knew they were in the presence of a genius and legend in the making.

Backed by thundering drums and twisted shards of spiralling guitar, The Thora Hurd Experience gave yet another blistering performance of music that was post-modern, post-ironic and post-music.

Get real, popkids: THORA HURD IS ROCK.

Why then, they were playing second fiddle to that campus comic and no-hoper Jonny Diggs (or *Digby Johnson*, as those of us present on the first day of his InterPol course will always know him) and his band of half-wits is a mystery.

Mercifully, only a couple of songs into their set, gig opener Curse-Tea brilliantly deconstructed Digby's feeble outpourings with her stage invasion and re-casting of the Bassey standard 'Big Spender' as 'Big Member', much to the deserved embarrassment of the headline band. The on-stage scuffle that followed was a clear visual indicator – if any were needed!!! – of the forces of radicalism triumphing over the conservatives, leaving only chaos in its wake.

Wise up, Digby, and make way for the new order. Curse-Tea and Thora are NOW. Big Member are YESTERDAY.

6. Don't Say You Love Me

5' 57" No, say it, baby, say it! Say it!

Alone on the platform at Ely station, the enormity of what I am doing hits me. I always told people that I would never go back; that it would take something very drastic to make me darken those horizons again. The Arctic Circle would melt first. Britain would become joined to the mainland. Madonna would put her clothes back on and start singing covers of old Don McLean songs. It was never likely to happen.

But here I am. Five and a half hours away from Aberystwyth and only three hours away from my home town. For a moment I grip the bench and have to physically restrain myself from turning around and getting right back on to a train to Birmingham. I don't know why I feel like this. Nothing bad ever happened to me there. But then again, nothing very interesting ever happened either and I grew up waiting for the day when I could get out and as soon as I could, I did. When family members listened to my determined promises to stay away and dared to ask me why, I could only scowl and say that the town was 'tedious' – a harsh judgement indeed from a girl who had rarely ventured outside her bedroom. But looking back on it all now, I realise that I gave them the right combination of letters but in the wrong order. It wasn't so much tedious as *outside*. Outside London, outside Ipswich and on the outside of anywhere interesting. At the age of eighteen and dressed dourly in a *Queen is Dead* T-shirt while everyone else had spiral perms (for her) or back perms (for him), it may just as well have been on the outside edge of the world to me.

The one redeeming feature was the record shop. Whereas any bigger, better place would have been blessed with an HMV megastore, we learned to make do with our very own GMV in the High Street. Gordon's Music and Video. Gordon was a heavy man in his mid-thirties who habitually wore eyeliner and repeatedly claimed that he had once appeared on Top of the Pops as a member of Captain Sensible's backing band. He was our very own homegrown Richard Branson and GMV was his empire. It was a tiny shop packed full of plastic-wrapped vinyl and patchouli-scented goths in bondage gear. In reality, there were only a couple of goths who lived in the town at that time but as the shop was so tiny and they were always in it, they were enough to pack it out. I knew both of them. Simon, the skinny goth, had been in my year at school and lent me his Sisters of Mercy album once when we were in the sixth-form together. In return, I had lent him *Treasure* by the Cocteau Twins but when he had returned it to me, I noticed that he had left fingerprints all over the vinyl so after that I never lent him anything else. His friend Malcolm, otherwise known around town as Fat Goth, worked in the food section of Marks and Spencers. He was big enough to crowd out GMV all on his own. I got to know these two and Gordon pretty well because I spent the best part of every Saturday afternoon browsing through the racks. That little shop sold every type of rock album you could want. Each rack was classified with a hand-written label so you could easily find exactly what you were after. Classic Rock. Glam Rock. Goth Rock. Heavy Rock. And if Gordon didn't have it, he would order it. All of the greatest conversations of my formative years were held in that shop.

'Who's best? The Mission or Sisters of Mercy?'

'The Bunnymen or The Commotions?'

'The Rolling Stones or Ned's Atomic Dustbin?'

Simon, Malcolm and I debated these issues long and hard every Saturday afternoon and Gordon would occasionally chip in with opinions of his own and never minded that we rarely had the money to buy anything from him. I loved that shop.

Sitting alone on the platform at Ely Station, I wait for my connecting train and smile.

I never questioned my decision to study in Aberystwyth until after I had gained my degree. For three years I had fielded the usual comments from condescending peers with

125

good grace and confidence and thrived in the knowledge that I was part of a lucky and elite group of English infiltrators who had discovered the secret of the most elusive and wonderful university campus in the whole of Great Britain. So what if we had no department stores, escalators or double-decker buses....

But after I graduated and all my friends had left to go back home and find themselves jobs, I found myself questioning the logic that had brought me from one side of the edge of the world to the other. Without a huge gang of friends and a course to attend, there seemed little to hold me in Aberystwyth. The maze of terraced streets which fanned out from the town and the bay now housed only memories. I felt like I was living in a town full of ghosts. Yet I still didn't want to go home. Neither did Jonny. Things had never been the same for his band since that fateful night up in the Student Union but he still felt that there was 'at least one good album in him waiting to get out'. So with this in mind, we moved out of the big student house on Llanbadarn Road and rented a one-bedroom flat on North Parade. Just the two of us and his guitars – all grown-up and cosy. And there, together, we had clung on to our safe and studentish existence and drunk in The Cambrian with the other remaining ghosts who floated with us in our beautiful Aber limbo.

The sun is high in the sky when I leave Ely. Train number three is short and shabby and reminds me very much of the one that took me out of Aberystwyth so many hours earlier. Aberystwyth already seems like another world to me and the people I encountered on that first train are carrying on their lives in a totally different dimension to the one I am in now. Newton Spots is walking around a university campus and counting the number of days left before he can leave Newtown forever. Mrs T Roberts of Borth is full of optimism and refusing to be dragged down by dreary letters about legal expenses. I wonder where she is now and what she can see from her window. I look out of mine and take in the endless horizons of The Fens.

Aberystwyth *looked* like another world compared to this. Perhaps my train has headed down the wrong track and I am now on the surface of the moon. In the distance I can see black smoke rising in a straight line. I focus my eyes and make out three figures standing around a fire onto which they are throwing car tyres. The whole scene is reflected on the watery surface of the black marshland and looks like the type of earthy, arty shot that might be found on the cover of a mid-Seventies Wings album. Only bleaker. More Smouldering Car Tyre than *Mull of Kintyre*. I stare out of the window and despite the force of the engine pulling me towards the east and the force of my own convictions to begin looking ahead, I find myself drifting through the miles and the hours back to Aberystwyth. I'm glad I finally found the strength to leave but there is one thing at least that I would have liked to resolve. Did Paul McCartney *really* own that music shop at the bottom of Penglais Hill?

Jonny liked definite endings. He told people this in his own inimitable and eloquent style and his wording was identical on each occasion. 'With a definite end, you know where you stand. The song is over, leaving your audience with no time to recover or reflect beyond the fact that whatever it was that they were listening to has now, very abruptly, gone. This means that the sense of loss is greater and your audience is more likely to beg for more. Fade-outs weaken that hunger. No Kurt Cobain song ever ends on a fade-out.'

It hit him quite hard then when the life of his own band, once seemingly destined for marvellous things, limped and crawled for several months and then, finally, petered out so indistinctly that barely anyone even noticed they had gone. Not even all the band members seemed aware that anything significant about their lives had altered. The passing of (Aberystwyth's) Mr Big could have been the most murky and nebulous affair to ever attract the town's attention. Except that it didn't. It was without doubt a most definite fade-out. Despite Jonny's best efforts to make it otherwise.

On stage at the Up Top Rock Night – or the Up Top Flop Night as it became known in Aber legend – they'd lost something and never managed to get themselves back together again. The name was the most apparent difficulty. With memories of Curse-Tea's stinging rendition of Hey Big Member stamped indelibly on Jonny's forehead, he refused to ever refer to his band by that name again. But with the LA claimant to the moniker following up their hit single *To Be With You* with another mushy slushy and enormously popular soft-rock ballad called *Just Take My Heart*, it was also apparent that this name too was unavailable for them to use. Unable to decide on anything else, they stayed nameless, and nameless, they pretty soon became gigless. At first, this lack of live bookings didn't worry Jonny; he just told people that he and the boys were using the next few months to 'gather new material'. I was happy to leave him to his songwriting and daydreaming. I'd managed to get myself a full-time job working as a junior librarian in the university's Hugh Owen Building and living without the stresses and strains of attending student rock gigs in seedy gaffs at the drop of a hat was a welcome relief to me. I could see that the band's days were numbered even if Jonny couldn't, and secretly I was not sorry. It meant that I might have him to myself for once.

The crunch came when Jeremy packed up his drums in the Mercedes Benz and drove off home to Hemel Hempstead. I had been walking down from the library when I saw the car travelling towards me in the opposite direction. Even without its former triangles, it was still very easy to spot. As far as I was aware, there weren't any other hand-painted 1977 Mercedes Benz being driven about Aberystwyth. The car – well into the winter of its life – was labouring and backfiring as it struggled up the one-in-four gradient. I waved and then stopped dead in my tracks as Jeremy's isolated middle finger appeared from the side window and pointed rigidly skyward. It didn't take a certificate in International Sign Language to work out that this was not a friendly response. Puzzled, I turned and watched the car disappear over the brow of the hill. Besides the usual jumble of snares and cymbals, I noticed bags and boxes were obscuring the view through the back window. Perhaps this was just another mission for The Gig Machine? I frowned, raised my own middle finger as a rather belated and feeble response and resumed my trudge down the hill. That was the last any of us ever saw of Jeremy.

Several weeks later he sent Jonny a letter. Jonny picked it up off the doormat, took one look at the Hemel Hempstead postmark and summoned Rhys, Waggy and Cefyn around to the house before solemnly reading the letter aloud.

> *Jonny,*
>
> *I thought I should write and let you know that I no longer wish to be the drummer in your band – if you still have a band, that is.*

'Ha, that's good of him to tell us. And there was me thinking he might want to commute to rehearsals.'

> *When we first got together, it was great and I really enjoyed myself but just like The Rolling Stones said in '65,* It's All Over Now.

'1965? I think he'll find it was 1964, actually.'

> *I have been less than happy in the band for a while but I feel that things really reached an all time low this past year.*

'All time low? He broke my fucking nose!'

You have never been at all supportive of me having a more creative role in the band and the hostility you have shown towards my appreciation of jazz is something that has been causing resentment in me for quite some time.

'Because jazz is shit, that's why.'

The final straw for me is the way that you deliberately attacked me in the full glare of the public at our last gig. My dad says I'm well within my rights to pursue a charge of assault against you.

'Assault! He broke my fucking nose!'

Worse than any injuries you inflicted upon me that night is the humiliation I endured in front of the eyes of strangers. I thought you were supposed to be my friend, Jonny.

'Friend? I'd rather saw my right arm off with a butter knife than be friends with that dickhead.'

I feel that you have forced me out of the band. Even without my dad's generous offer to pay off my student loans on the condition that I cut my hair and live back at home, I know that I would have made the same progressive decision anyway. Please apologise to the

*others for my abrupt departure. After all, if anyone is to
do any apologising it ought be you.*

No more hard feelings,

Jeremy

'No more hard feelings? I hope his co-ordination goes
up the spout and his hands fall off.'

Jonny put the letter down on the table. The rest of us
sat in total silence. Jonny smoothed the letter out with his
hands, tapped some tobacco on to the middle of it and then
proceeded to turn the whole thing into a giant spliff. We all
watched with mounting interest. Jonny twisted the edges
into a tight coil and then picked it up carefully.

'I am going to smoke this letter as a sign of my total
and utter contempt. It was full of shit anyway, so it seems
only fitting.'

Briefly, I wondered if I should try to stop him. He was
depressed enough at the moment. I didn't want him to get
pleurisy on top of everything else. I looked at Jonny's face.
His broken nose was creased at the bridge in a snarl and
his jaw was set in a stubborn sulk. Something told me I
should leave him to it. Jonny raised the creation to his
lips, struck a match and ignited the end. A small flame
tentatively licked the edges of the paper, liked it, and then
seared upwards in a ferocious eruption of gluttony. The
full-of-shit spliff was completely consumed and all that
Jonny achieved was the instant loss of a few grams of his
precious gear and the near-incineration of our living-room
table. If it hadn't been for the presence of Rhys and his

adeptness at extinguishing flames with his bare body parts, we may well have had to enlist the services of the boys in the big red *Tân Sir Dyfed* van.

'Seems to me that Rizla papers exist for a reason,' was all Rhys had to say about the event once the immediate danger had passed.

Like I said before, for all his charm and good looks, Jonny could be a bit of a prat sometimes. It's just taken me a long while to acknowledge it.

Somewhere between Bury St Edmunds and Stowmarket, I am approached by a ticket inspector. Despite the length of my journey, he is the first ticket inspector I have encountered. When he makes his way into my carriage, I am pleased to see him because I was beginning to believe that I may just as well have done this journey illegally and saved myself a whopping £104.50 in the process.

I take my well-travelled ticket out of my purse and pass it over to the inspector. He is a cheery-looking man in his fifties who has been making jovial small talk with all the passengers as he passes. I feel an overwhelming urge to say something, *anything*, to this man. It has now been so long since I last spoke that I am beginning to wonder if my voice still works. I smile and clear my throat in preparation for a friendly exchange. He takes my ticket and glances at it. As he does so, his eyebrows rise dramatically.

'You've come all the way from Aberystwyth have you? Crikey, that's a long journey, my dear. You must have got up early this morning.'

I'm about to say something back to him which will

confirm that indeed, he is right; I did get up very early this morning. Unfortunately I don't get my words out quick enough.

'Never have been to Aberystwyth myself,' he says, and pauses to punch a hole through my ticket. 'The wife never fancied Scotland.'

He hands me back the dog-eared piece of card and smiles. The opportunity is now there for me to speak if I like but the inclination has passed. I smile and say nothing.

Rhys was the next one to deliver a body blow to the band. He appeared at the front door suspiciously early one Sunday morning and told Jonny that he had something important to tell him.

'Bonnie Tyler got a new record coming out?' Jonny joked, but I noticed that he wasn't grinning. He had guessed what was coming just as clearly as I had.

'No... at least, I don't think she has,' answered Rhys with a frown. 'Mind you, I haven't really heard anything much of her since she put out that single *Holding Out For a Hero* so it's probably high time she did release something else. I think I might nip down to Andy's Records and ask him if...'

'Rhys!' Jonny raised his hand and made a stop signal as if he was a lolly-pop man. Rhys looked at him in surprise. 'Rhys, I couldn't really give a toss about Bonnie Tyler. You're leaving the band, aren't you?'

Rhys looked down at his feet and shifted them uncomfortably. His silence told us everything. Confused, I left the room and went into the kitchen to put the kettle

134

on and give myself some space to think. Part of me felt that it was time Jonny moved on. He couldn't cling to the security blanket of his band forever. However, another part of me felt angered that Rhys could dare to be one of the first to depart. I poured three cups of coffee and very dangerously managed to carry all three at once back into the living room.

Jonny and Rhys were now sitting down. Rhys was still looking uncomfortable. Jonny was looking eerily calm. He gave Rhys a sad philosophical smile. 'It's alright, mate. I don't blame you really. We've got no drummer and no name and it doesn't take a genius to work out that while that situation remains, we're going nowhere fast. Have you found another band?'

Encouraged, Rhys perked up a little in his chair. 'Yeah, well, I've been asked to play guitar in this new band. It's Welsh punk. I think that Welsh punk could just be on the up you know. Those Manic Street Preachers from Blackwood have been in the Top Forty all year. We want to be a little bit like them but Welsh language. We could go down a storm. I reckon we're probably a bit more talented than they are, as well.'

My heart sank. It sounded as if Rhys was definitely leaving. If Jonny was at all upset by the enthusiasm that Rhys was showing for his new project, he manfully refused to let it show. 'That sounds cool, Rhys. What are you called? I'll look out for you in the NME.'

'*Y Ceseiliau*. It can mean either The Armpits or The Breasts. Whatever body part takes your fancy the most. I know which I prefer.'

135

Jonny smiled. 'Either way, it's better than any of the names we thought of. Good luck mate.'

'Thanks.' Rhys extended his arm and the two solemnly shook hands. 'I've learned loads from being in Mr Big and I had a really good time as well but it just sort of feels right to move on now. And Cefyn's songs sound great; I think this could really...'

Jonny dropped Rhys' hand. 'Cefyn's songs sound great? What the hell do you mean, *Cefyn's songs sound great?*'

Rhys blushed and looked at me for support. I glared back at him.

'Well... *Y Ceseiliau*... it was all Cefyn's idea.'

'So he's leaving us as well, is he?'

'Well, he was never *really* in, was he? You never really needed a French Horn player.'

Jonny opened his mouth and for a moment I thought that he might actually try to convince Rhys that Cefyn's French Horn playing had always been a vital component of the sound he'd been striving to create, but he thought better of it and instead smirked at Rhys maliciously. 'So you're joining a Welsh punk band with a theology student who plays the French Horn. That's really fucking avant-garde that is. That'll have them spitting in the Union.'

'He's not going to be playing the French Horn. He's our singer actually. And he's written some really good lyrics too.'

'Ha!' Jonny glared triumphantly. 'How do you know they're any good? You don't speak Welsh, remember? He could be singing about taking tea with his Gran for all you know. You lot could be the Aled Joneses of the punk world. Cool. *Not!*'

Rhys stood glowering for a second and then marched towards the door. Before he left, he turned to give his final parting shot. 'Don't worry, Jonny. At least you're still in a band. *Not!*'

He disappeared and a second later, we heard the door slam. Jonny sank wearily on to the sofa. 'There's only me and Waggy left now.' He looked up at me in despair. 'What are we gonna do? Become Simon and Garfunkel?'

I stood still. The slam of the door was still echoing. 'I wish you hadn't been so shitty to Rhys. You can't blame him for wanting to try something else.'

Jonny shifted uncomfortably. 'I know. I'm just annoyed that he's been poached by Cefyn.' He sighed. 'It's my fault. I should never have given Cefyn a free hand to write 'Mr Morgan's Organ'. The power and ambition obviously went to his head. I've helped to create a monster. But I'll make it up with Rhys. I promise I will.'

And to his credit, he did make it up with Rhys. Within a few days, the row was forgotten and Jonny even found the good grace to wish Cefyn all the best with his newly found punk direction.

Which, as he said, just left him and Waggy. They didn't become Simon and Garfunkel. They decided instead to pursue their own solo careers. For Waggy, to the surprise of everyone who knew him, this meant joining Burger King as a trainee manager, where he was soon swapping humbuckers and pick-ups for hamburgers and ketchup.

But Jonny did not let go of his dreams so easily. 'The

137

thing is, babe,' he began one evening, during an earnest future-plotting discussion, 'there isn't anything else I'm any good at. I only want to do music. Nothing else appeals to me.'

I tried to reach a compromise. 'What about *selling* it instead? Maybe Andy's Records would take you on.'

Jonny wrinkled up his broken nose. 'No, you're missing the point a bit, babe. I've got a creative urge inside me. I need to make music. It's what I was put on this planet to do. I just feel wrong at the moment.'

'Then maybe you could join another band. Perhaps Rhys could...'

'Don't even go there!'

'Not The Comfy Chair!?'

'No point. They're going nowhere.'

'Thora Hurd Experience?' My eyes gleamed wickedly. I knew this was really pushing it but it was always amusing to wind Jonny up whenever I could. Too often, it happened the other way around. Jonny narrowed his eyes and threw a cushion at my head. I ducked. The cushion missed and crashed against a mug half-filled with day-old coffee. Jonny shook his head in mock exasperation and grabbed hold of my left ankle. 'Now look what you've made me do. I shall have to punish you, you wicked girl!' He then proceeded to torture me by tickling my bare foot. I squirmed hysterically and tried to kick him away but his grip on my ankle remained fast. 'Any more bright suggestions?'

'Leave me alone will you... arggh... er... The Killer Toasters?'

'They're rubbish.'

'Please stop it... pleeaaase... Hector's House?'

'Bunch of nutters.'

'I hate being tickled... ohhh... Heavysidz?'

Jonny instantly let go of my foot. 'Never *ever* mention that band to me again.'

The mood had changed. I sat up, red-faced, and rubbed my foot. I had unwisely forgotten that this was a taboo subject. I tried to think of something more constructive to say. 'Well, why don't you just go it alone then, Jon. You're a singer anyway, and you write the songs. What's stopping you?'

Jonny sighed. 'I don't know. I don't want to be known around Aber as some kind of Val Doonican character.'

I frowned. 'That's not very likely, Jonny. Val's sexy!'

'Right, that's it!' Jonny lunged forwards, sat heavily on my legs and closed his ears to my shrill protests as both of my feet were tortured simultaneously. Only when I threatened – very seriously – that I would wee myself, did he finally agree to stop. Fortunately for me, I had his jeans on.

I must have been dozing again. One second ago, I was adrift in a world which contained nothing more than the music of Catatonia, numb feet and a ridiculously uncomfortable seat. The next thing I know, I am leaping out of my seat in a hurry to get to the loo. I am dangerously close to what my mum used to refer to as a 'splash pants situation.' These are fair enough when you are three. Less so on your thirty-first birthday.

So, adrift and without a band, Jonny made the best of what seemed at the time to be a terrible situation and re-modelled himself as a solo artist. With my support and encouragement, he picked up his guitar again and sang along, accompanied only by himself. Some of the songs that he wrote alone in our flat, while I stamped the books of endless queues of students, were among the best and most beautiful that he had ever written. When his new repertoire was ready and his confidence was restored, he walked with his guitar to the bridge at Trefechan and played an acoustic set to a small but appreciative crowd in Rummers. Along with the handful of new songs that he had written, he played a few covers by Rod Stewart and Nick Drake and anything on the *Fire and Water* album by Free. They gave him a regular slot.

And in spite of my boredom with the books, and in defiance of the poverty I endured from keeping the two of us afloat on my solitary wage, I could have borne it all if life had stayed like that. I realise now that I should have heeded the signs. During those days alone in the flat, a change came over Jonny. His initial excitement at becoming a house regular at Rummers faded after only a couple of months. The impulsive and lively manner which had always endeared him to me so much became introverted and depressive. He started to snap at me in a way that he had never done before. 'This flat is shit,' he announced one day after I had come home from a long silent day in the library. 'You don't take enough pride in the place. My mum would freak if she saw the state of this living room.'

His words angered me. I might not have minded so

much but it was his stuff that was lying about everywhere. And that included his body too, which was pretty much a permanent fixture in front of the rented TV during daytime hours. I struck back. 'You're in all day so YOU clear it up! And for your information, it isn't me who leaves beer bottles and crisp packets everywhere.' I stormed into the one bedroom so that I could get away from him but before I slammed the door firmly between him and me, I added, 'Go and shack up with Delia Smith if it's a nice little wife you're after.'

That row blew itself out but Jonny remained changed. His face grew drawn, and even his beautiful blond hair, once so long and so lustrous, eventually succumbed to the dissatisfied voices which were whispering to him from inside. One morning, I went to work knowing that I had a boyfriend with long rock hair and by the time I got home, I found he had been replaced with a serious looking man who wore a severe but serviceable crop. This serious short-haired stranger was sat on the floor of the living-room sorting his records into various carrier bags when I entered the flat.

'What have you done to your hair? I exclaimed and then, before he could answer, followed it up with, 'What are you doing to your records?'

His answers were terse and frighteningly cogent. 'I've had a haircut, *obviously*, because I can't look like a slob all my life. And I'm sorting out some records to sell. I don't need all of these. There are loads I hardly ever listen to.'

I stared at him confused. Was he telling me then that Paul Kossoff and Paul Rodgers and Marc Bolan were all slobs? And since when did anyone only ever keep the records that they *needed?* I didn't *need* any of my records. Especially *No Parlez* by Paul Young. But even that one, I had been unable to part with. My records, good or bad, the object of glowing pride or acute embarrassment, seemed to be a living document of who I was. At that moment, I knew that something very bad was happening. I didn't like this shorthaired impostor; I wanted Jonny back. I braced myself for the worst and demanded that he tell me exactly what was wrong.

'I'm bored here,' he said.

I tried to get him to go to the pub with me so that we could talk things through over a pint or two but Jonny, who had cut down on his drinking since he had seen the effect it had had on Curse-Tea and her band, declined. I then tried to get him to talk to me in the flat but to my horror, I discovered that Jonny was beyond talking anything over. He had been *making plans*. Plans that didn't include me.

'I need to grow up,' he said. 'I can't hang around here forever sponging off you. I need to earn my own money.'

'So get a job then.'

'There aren't any jobs here. I don't want to end up making burgers like Waggy.'

'But *I* found a decent job. You can find a job, Jonny.'

'I already have.'

'Well then that's great. What's the problem then?'

'It's in Portsmouth.'

'Portsmouth?'

'Yeah... my mum sorted it for me really but I had an interview last time I was home and I've been mulling it over for a while.'

'Portsmouth?'

'I could live with my parents for a bit and get some money together and pay off a few of my debts.'

'Portsmouth?'

'It's working for the Tax Inspectorate. I'd never get a job like that here.'

'The Tax Inspectorate? But what about your music?

'You know I think I'm through with music now. It's been such great fun in Aberystwyth but let's face it, I'm never going to be Jimi Hendrix, am I? I'm not even going to be Shakin' Stevens at this rate.'

Panic welled. 'What about me, Jonny? You should have told me about this before. I'll have to serve out my notice at the library. I've got ties here now. I can't just up and leave straight away with you.'

Jonny turned red and looked at the floor. I waited in mounting horror and wished that I could stop the world from spinning.

'I'm ready to move on. I need... well... you belong here. I don't anymore. We're both so young. Too young, really. My mum and dad think... I'm going to live at home with them. It's not a very big house.' My jaw had gone all numb. I felt like I was going to be sick. Jonny looked up but his eyes were unable to meet mine. 'Part of me will always love you, you know that, don't you?'

Part of him would always love me? *Part of him?* Which part? Was I supposed to make-do with this arrogant man's big toe? Or did he mean his *big member?* Actually, it wasn't all that big, now that I thought about it. That whole band name thing had been a sham. But this was no joke. My stupor was broken. I placed my hands over my ears and shooting him a look full of fury, I rose stiffly from my seat, and left. I didn't want to hear him say that. He had no right to even dare to say that. It was just his selfish way of easing his conscience and I was not going to allow it. Way down inside, I knew that nothing I could say would stop him from leaving and I needed to find a way to learn to stop loving him. And then I could get on with my life.

Three days later, Jonny got up really early and caught the first train out of Aber that would take him on his long journey towards the south coast. As far as me and the rock band Free were concerned, that was the day the music died.

7. All Right Now

5' 31" The best feel good track ever written. Ever...!

It is nearly two o'clock when the train pulls in at Ipswich Station. I am almost nine hours adrift of my hypnotic and hibernating Aber existence. My journey will soon be over. I have gone West Coast to East Coast. Just like Tupac Shakur, only I hope that I will fare a bit better than he did. I feel my consciousness stirring. As the train slows, I am able to look once again on scenes which have been imprinted on my mind since childhood. Children playing on the swings on Borne Park. The floodlights of Portman Road Football Ground. The sinister stuff which falls out of the pipe at the back of the abattoir along the side of the railway track. It is still falling in just the same way that it was thirteen years ago when I first sat here on my way home for an official mid-term reading week; a fresher besotted with a boy who drove a clapped-out and customised Mercedes Benz. A lamb to the slaughter myself. Only, *I* am able to have my life back again... even if I have had to wait nine years to get it. The stuff coming from the pipe does not have the same possibilities. I know a lot of people who have turned vegetarian because of looking at that pipe. I look at the pipe again and realise that I am starving. I think about hamburgers.

However, I have no time to buy a hamburger or anything else because I have only ten minutes to wait until my train leaves for Felixstowe and I don't want to miss it because the next one doesn't leave for another hour. I take my seat on this new train and listen to some more Catatonia to try to lessen the sudden pain that I am feeling. There is something very soothing about the Welsh lilt of Cerys Matthews' voice. It is as if I have brought a tiny part of Wales back home with me. Beginning this new life is not at all easy. Maybe that's why I delayed for so long.

My mum has no idea that her prodigal daughter is now only thirty minutes away from home and in need of indefinite board and lodging. I try to picture her face when she takes the phone call that will tell her I am in Felixstowe town centre and would appreciate a lift if she's not too busy. She will be almost as surprised as I am. I should perhaps have forewarned her of my intentions but how could I? I only knew myself that I was very probably coming home when I walked out of my job at the library and booked my ticket at the train station and that was just four days ago. And in the days that followed, I didn't dare say anything just in case I changed my mind again. In one of those parallel universes that beckon me at every turn, I know that I traded the ticket in for another with a completely unknown destination and chanced my luck somewhere else entirely. I look out of the window and watch as the back yards of Ipswich scroll past me. A mother hangs out her washing whilst her little boy waves cheerily at the train which runs along the back wall of his garden. I wave back and am suddenly struck with a sense of how extraordinary the likelihood of this interaction is. Where would I normally be at this time on a Saturday afternoon? Drinking tea in Caffi Morgan or drinking gin in The Cambrian, depending on how rough I am feeling the day after the night before. I will have to find out new haunts now and new ghosts to haunt with. Perhaps, if I am very lucky, I will be able to step out from the shadows altogether and burn a little more brightly.

There are only a handful of us on this train. It appears that very few people ever want to go right to the end of the line. Maybe they are afraid of what they might find there. I have travelled from one end of the line to the other but as yet I have not found what I am looking for. I am close to it though. I can feel that much inside me.

For the second time, I am approached by a ticket inspector and I reach for my ticket and feel a little glow of satisfaction which comes with the knowledge that I have really got my money's worth out of his ilk today. This inspector looks like he should have been pensioned off years ago; he looks old enough to be my grandfather. I hand him the ticket and, just like his predecessor, his eyebrows reach the top of his very wrinkly forehead. I wait for the inevitable. He holds the ticket at arm's length and tilts it slightly to check that he hasn't misread *Aberystwyth* for something more expected, like *Manningtree* or *Colchester*.

'Ab-o-wrist-worth,' he says slowly. 'Ab-o-wrist-worth ta Phil-licks-toe. You don't get too many o tham ta the pound now, do yah?' He is not looking at me; he is still looking at the ticket. He does not expect me to answer so I don't. I just wait patiently to hear what will come next. A few seats further up, a middle-aged woman is now listening to the ticket inspector with interest and regarding me suspiciously as if I were some kind of freak. An Ab-o-wrist-worth kind of freak.

'Would that be hin tha' prorximity of Clan-dud-noo? I can't say as how I've ever bin to Ab-o-wrist-worth but I have bin ta Clan-dud-noo on occasion.'

I give the old man a half shake of my head – half shrug. I can't be too hard on him. He is, at least, referring to the right part of Britain and hasn't fallen into the usual trap of confusing Aberystwyth with Aberdeen or Abu-Dhabi.

'And I can tal yoo somp'n fa noth'n. I've bin ta Phil-licks-toe on many an occasion,' he says and cackles happily at his own wit. He punches my ticket and moves on to the next passenger. I reach for the volume control of my walkman and flick Catatonia back up to maximum but not before I hear the ticket man say, 'Ah, that's more loike 't. An Anglia Roover ticket. Now, I know where it is I am with a ticket loike thairrt.'

I put my ticket back into my purse and hope that I haven't upset the rhythm of his day too much.

The train is moving through familiar parts of Ipswich

now. We have passed through Westerfield and we are just passing the car scrap-yard at Derby Road. Once, when I was an introverted and painfully miserable sixteen year old, I sat on this very same train and wrote a poem about the scrap-yard at Derby Road, only I called my poem 'Derby Junction' because I thought that the word *junction* added more of a railway feel. The Derby Junction of my poem was a very different place from the *Dyfi* Junction I would later become acquainted with. But curiously, although it was undoubtedly a much dirtier place, I never had any hang-ups about breathing in this place. I can still remember the poem and I silently recite it to myself as we leave the precarious piles of cars behind.

Derby Junction

Heaps of tangled metal
Slowly eat the foliage
Private cars and rental
No longer clocking up mileage
And as I sat and pondered
Sixteen, withdrawn and depressed
I saw that like the motor cars
So were my dreams compressed.

Fortunately, by the time I was seventeen, I had gained enough self-awareness to realise that I must knock the poetry on the head and destroy all my notebooks before anyone chanced upon them.

The train is picking up speed now – we must be

chugging along at an exhilarating forty miles per hour at least. Ipswich is now behind and we are cutting through the expanse of ramshackle farms and fields that separate that town from Felixstowe. The final frontier. A small town at the end of the line on the edge of the sea. So like Aber and yet so absolutely completely different in every way. My mother especially could never understand why I decided to stay on living there, after college and after Jonny. And how could I explain to her that aside from lethargy and laziness, it was all about ice-pops.

Ice-pops? It is 1977, the year of the Queen's Silver Jubilee. I am six years old and on holiday with my family who are staying in a hired holiday cottage in Bethesda. Bethesda, a place of extraordinary beauty, the Welsh language and the Meibion Glyndŵr who burn down the summer retreats of holidaying *Saeson*. Several years later, my parents told me that they went off Wales that summer because everywhere we went, people had insisted on speaking to each other in Welsh. So unfriendly! But their complaints against these people were lost on me. We had been in Wales. What did they expect them to speak? Turkish?

At six years old in Bethesda, I found this strange, baffling means of communication a pleasing curiosity. The more I listened, the less I understood and the more intrigued I was. A fascination for all things Welsh grew inside me. I became a sympathiser, an enemy infiltrator. And why? Because in the face of the apparent hostility arrowed at my parents, there lived next door to our rented holiday cottage an ancient and kindly monoglot called

Mrs Williams who popped her head over the garden fence whenever I was playing on the swing and wordlessly handed me ice-pops with a smile. My mother asked me where the ice-pops had come from and I told her they were from the old lady next door.

'Are you sure? I don't think she really speaks any English.'

'Well she still gives me ice-pops,' I replied with a six year old's shrug.

And since that dim and distant childhood holiday, whenever I have thought of Wales, I have thought of the generosity of Mrs Williams who instilled in me at a young age the wisdom that Welshness has nothing to do with the burning down of holiday homes.

How could I explain to my mum that ice-pops were a major factor in making me, a Felixstowe girl, choose Aberystwyth as a place to study? Ice-pops and the fact that it was a very very long way away from Felixstowe.

On the skyline appear the monstrous outlines of cranes and containers: the biggest container port in Europe. Or, as the local teenagers like to proudly boast, 'the biggest *fucking* container port in Europe.' Every now and then, I catch a glimpse of the twinkling grey expanse of the North Sea and each time this happens, I feel my heart beat slightly faster. If I stare at it hard enough, I can see myself drinking a Stella in Blankenberge or Knokke against a backdrop of the same shimmering grey void. If I want to go further, I can reach out and shake hands with the people who live along the Baltic and anytime I want, I can always follow the waves south, squeeze myself through the English

Channel, float in the vastness of the Atlantic Ocean and then push my way upwards to Cardigan Bay. I had always thought that the sea was hemming me in, but this realisation invigorates me.

We pass through the mostly modern built village of Trimley and, much slower now, roll by the playing fields of the school where I endured seven deliriously dull years as a pupil. As the train comes to the end of its journey, I find I am holding my breath again. The train halts with a slight jolt and along with the handful of other passengers on the train, I alight. I take my bag and my rucksack and finally, permanently step forward on to a solid surface.

The clock in Great Eastern Square tells me that it is two thirty-five or as the people around here would prefer to tell me *five and twenty to three*. I get a better grip on my bags and march through the square, turning right at the top. Deliberately, I ignore the payphones as I walk by because I am not yet quite ready to ring my mum. Before I go home, there is something that I need to do. Something that I *must* do if I am to begin my life again successfully. Still struggling under the weight of my bags, I make my way down Hamilton Road and keep my mind clearly targeted on my purpose. People may be watching me as I stride by because, despite being the opposite end of a line, Felixstowe is not a mirror image of Aberystwyth. There are no people like Jonny or Curse-Tea or Borth Woman here and unless the population has changed, there aren't too many people like me either. It is not normal to see people with rucksacks walking through the centre of Felixstowe. Such behaviour is a clear indication of deviance. Undaunted, I continue and hope against hope that just for once, I will find what I am looking for.

To my joy, it is still there. Admittedly, it has changed hands and the décor outside is now a disturbing combination of red and black paint-work, but these are just cosmetic details. Essentially, it is as it was. It is no longer called GMV; it has changed its name to S and M Records. Risqué. I push open the door and enter the darkness of the little shop. Behind the counter sits a painfully thin man about the same age as me. His hair, as thin on his head as the body attached to that head, is blue-black and he is wearing a washed-out looking All About Eve T-shirt. I recognise him at once.

'Simon! What the hell are you doing behind that counter?'

Simon puts down his copy of *Mojo* and peers at me closely for a moment before breaking into a delighted beaming smile which is curiously at odds with his shadowy persona.

'Ally! What the hell are you doing *that* side of the counter? The last I heard, you were living up in Aberdeen. Long time no see, Al.'

It is wonderful to stand in this strange little shop and hear my name spoken aloud. I am injected with life and confidence. 'I've come home,' I tell him in a rush. Now that I'm able to use my voice again, I can't seem to get my words out quick enough. 'I mean, I'm home for good. I'm going to live with my mum for a bit and then see if I can get a job or something.'

'Cool,' says Simon. 'Maria will be pleased. I'll have to

introduce you. She's always moaning about how this town's full of nobody but pensioners.'

'Maria?'

'The wife. I've got kids too. Three of them. Kayleigh, Eloise and Andrew. All named after various gems from my record collection.'

My mind races. 'Kayleigh after the song by Marillion.'

Simon smiles. 'Of course.'

'Eloise from the song by The Damned.'

'Well it was originally a hit for Barry Ryan in 1968 but I'll let you have it. And Andrew?'

I shake my head, beaten. My brain is finding it hard enough to cope with the idea that he's found the time to produce three kids. Am I that old?

Simon explains. 'We couldn't think of a song we both liked that had a boy's name in it. So I named him Andrew after Andrew Eldritch in the Sisters of Mercy. I really wanted to just call him Eldritch but Maria wouldn't let me.'

I am reminded of Simon's surname. 'Eldritch Aldridge wouldn't sound that good.'

Simon laughs. 'It would have been character building. Not that he'll need it. Being the son of the sole-surviving goth in Felixstowe should test him enough.'

A thought strikes me. 'What happened to your friend, Malcolm?'

'Malc? Oh, he's still around. But he's in the Police Force now. That required a little bit of an image change. Anyway, was there anything you were looking for today, Al? Anything I can help you with?'

'Yes, actually.' I open up my bag, rummage around

near the bottom and pull out something which I offer to Simon. 'I don't suppose you've got a decent copy of this on vinyl, have you?'

Simon frowns. 'May have. Second hand. It's a bit of a while since I sorted through some of that stuff but it's worth a look.'

I move over to a corner of the shop labelled *Classic Rock* and begin to rummage. As I search, I see many things which I would quite like to buy on another occasion when I have more cash with me but today, there is only one thing I am after. I flick over *F* after *F*. Fairport Convention. Mimi Farina. Fleetwood Mac. Focus. Foreigner. And then, just as I am beginning to lose faith, I find it. Neither signed nor faded but wonderful all the same. *Fire and Water* by Free. I pull it out from the rack and hold it in my trembling hands. Hardly daring to breathe, I slide the record out of its inner and outer sleeves and, taking care not to place my thumbs on the black vinyl, tilt the album towards the shop window. The light bounces off the black surface and reveals a shining and unblemished finish. Side A and Side B are both flawless. The Island logos on either side of the record are wonderfully appropriate. A perfect sunrise and a perfect sunset. I breathe out again with relief and, after replacing the record in its sleeve, I take it to Simon at the counter.

'You had it!'

He takes the album from me and turns it over in his hands. '*All Right Now*. That's a great track. You know they should have called that song Fucking Brilliant Now.'

'Exactly,' I reply, suddenly feeling elated.

He puts the album into a red and black S and M Records carrier bag for me.

'Don't forget this,' he says waving Jonny's hand-taped cassette copy which I have not allowed myself to listen to for nine years.

'Stick it in the bin,' I reply with a casual wave of the hand. 'I don't need it anymore.'

'Come in again, Ally. It's really good to see you back. You should meet Maria.'

I smile.

'See you later, then.'

'Later.'

Still smiling, I leave his shop and head back for Great Eastern Square, the sun shining brightly over Hamilton Road and my copy of *Fire and Water* tucked under my arm.

I'm ready to listen to it again.

ALWAYS YOU

Caroline Khoury

PENGUIN BOOKS

PENGUIN BOOKS

UK | USA | Canada | Ireland | Australia
India | New Zealand | South Africa

Penguin Books is part of the Penguin Random House group of companies
whose addresses can be found at global.penguinrandomhouse.com

Penguin
Random House
UK

Published in Penguin Books 2023
001

Copyright © Caroline Khoury, 2023

The moral right of the author has been asserted

Typeset in 10/15.2 pt Palatino LT Std
by Integra Software Services Pvt. Ltd, Pondicherry

Printed and bound in Great Britain by Clays Ltd, Elcograf S.p.A.

The authorised representative in the EEA is Penguin Random House
Ireland, Morrison Chambers, 32 Nassau Street, Dublin D02 YH68

A CIP catalogue record for this book is available from the British Library

ISBN: 978–1–52915–935–6

www.greenpenguin.co.uk